Alexandra

J. M. Mitchell

Published by J. M. Mitchell, 2023.

ALEXANDRA

First edition. April 28, 2023.

ISBN: 979-8223510581

Written by J. M. Mitchell.

"He makes me feel small and soft like a baby animal under the large, leafed branches of a tall tree, hiding from the rain."

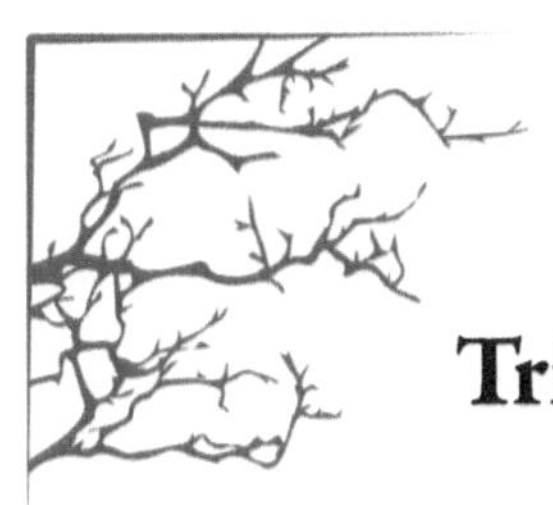

Trigger Warning:

Mild Sexual Assault
Songs:
Fall For Me – Sleep Token
Monsters – Meg & Dia
Long Live The Chief – Jidenna

- Slainte

The Accountant

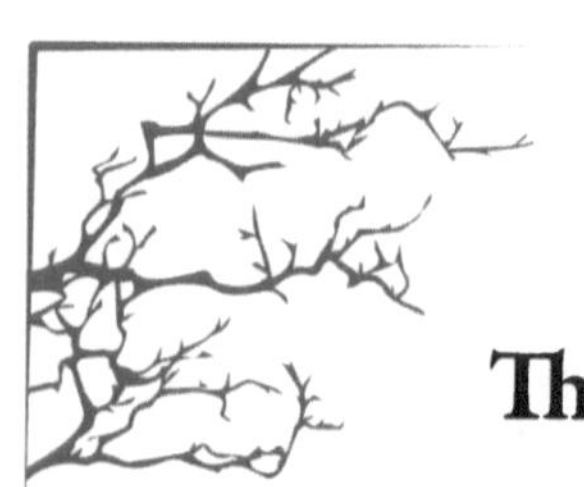

Luckily sleep came easy last night, only one nightmare woke me, from which I was able to fall back asleep in less than an hour. I pat around the bed for my phone without moving my body, eyes glued shut, until my fingers graze its corner. Unable to grip the small nook between the case and the screen I offer a silent whine to the morning like a child mad at the sun. I turn my palm up and slide my middle finger under my phone throwing it towards me a half centimeter at a time until I feel it the palm of my hand. I flop my back to the bed raising my arms, lifting my phone above my face. I need to check that Mrs. Hayes made her second payment. I'm not supposed to know her identity, those with her social standing prefer to remain anonymous, however she made it blaringly obvious in her emails, yes there was hurt and pain, but it scaled to disgust rather than vengeance. Mr. Tristan Hayes has been taking advantages with the nieces and nephews within his family tree for many years. Five hundred thousand, payment successful. Its pocket change to her and I know I could've charged more but I really don't do this for the money, plus keeping the charges low looks good on paper, my company gives me a lot of free reign but do I have people to answer to, and taxes to pay. Mrs. Hayes for example hired me to "find a large amount of funds missing from her overseas account", which according to my Master of Finance degree I have every right to charge a million dollars for. This also allows me to charge people like Mrs. Lawrence only fifty dollars for doing her taxes the year her new cop husband locked himself in the basement with her daughter to teach her a lesson after she spent the night with the high school playboy. The girl had to be hospitalized for months, unconscious, internal bleeding, broken ribs, while he reported "an unknown boyfriend" for the girl's condition. I wish I could say I did this with good intentions and a pure heart, a vigilante of justice, but the truth is this is just revenge, the little girl I never got to be is still hurt, broken, and pissed off, like Rorschach said "Dogs get put down".

I swipe the bank away up and out of sight, pull up the internet for a quick search on Tristan Hayes. I shot a few rounds into the air at one of the Hayes LLC construction sites just after midnight, cops should have responded within twenty minutes, plenty of time for some information to be circulating the news. They would have found Hayes hanging by his wrists, feet just an inch from the ground separated by an ankle spreader, a mirror in front of him, well flayed slivers of his skin circling the ground around him. The momentary distraction of his dangling body, skinned from the hips up broken by the realization that his pathetic excuse for a cock was zip tied tightly midshaft almost detaching it from his body, two sounders inserted at full depth, eroded from the lye that mixed with his blood. His autopsy will reveal he was raped, anally and orally, by a wooden bat and a shock stick, the same stick that radiated his skin so deeply it charred the muscle beneath. *Tristan Hayes found brutally slain in the early hours of the morning.* I don't bother clicking the link to the article, letting my limbs fall to the bed beside me, a hum of pride vibrating within me. I do need to get out of bed though, I can feel the hunger gnawing my stomach, my mind envisioning a pancake topped with fresh banana and whipped cream. *Yep, I'm hungry.* I roll my body out of the bed like it's too heavy to lift, my knees flopping to the ground, my face planted in the mattress stifling my annoyed groan. I jet my face to the ceiling, sighing as I press my hands against the mattress lifting my knees from the floor. *Fuck, all the way off. Damn it Alex.* The bedding is covered sporadically in blood, thank God I didn't sleep under the covers, I have no desire to process a mattress. I retrieve the bleach from my duffle, cinch the comforter in my arms and begin to shuffle my feet toward the bathroom, grabbing the red wine from the service cart on the way. I don't drink alcohol, but I've learned to always be prepared for blood and order it for these exact moments. I pull up the pin, spread the comforter out as best I can around the small tub, turn on the water and open the wine bottle, twisting off the cheaply made metal screw top. Shutting off the faucet I empty the bottle of bleach into the cold water letting it swirl and settle. I remove the well fitted black t shirt and jeans sticking to my skin like tape dropping them into the tub, then wipe the flaking blood from my skin and carelessly toss the washcloth in with the comforter and clothing. I shrug my shoulders, counting the steps across the open room to the chair before the window that's holding my bag, dressing in the same clothing I recently removed from body with the addition of socks, black of course, topped with white tennis sneakers. Returning to the bathroom, the burn in my lungs surprises me as I inhale the strength of the bleach, attempting to shoo it away with the waft of a hand, reaching down with my free hand I press the pin opening the drain, the gurgle of the water assaulting my senses, like an invisible hand clenching around my spine. I shake my limbs to rid the immediate discomfort as I reach for the wine bottle waiting on the counter. I watch the last of the water flow down the small hole, pouring the deep red liquid over the various textiles weighing down on themselves in the tub. I find myself annoyed with my own actions, it's not a hard task, it's not even tedious, I just hate doing it the way you hate folding the clothes you forgot to take out of the dryer the night before. *Time to go.* I grab up my duffle bag and place the do not disturb sign on the door as I pull it shut. French vanilla iced coffee, two pumps caramel, oat milk, and sweet cream cold foam, is tugging at my soul. Luckily I only live about five minutes away, with a coffee shop in route.

Stepping off the elevator I see none other than Ian Hayes, with three of his bodyguards looming around him. I wonder where the fourth is. I've learned Scarlett and Silver are referred to as The Boys, a term of endearment Scarlett doesn't seem to mind even though they are A-Gender. My brow raises at the androgyny dripping from them, my eyes drinking in the well fitted three-piece suit hugging their body I'd be all too happy to remove. A shoulder attempts to block my view, jetting my thoughts back to the real world. I let my eyes jump to the face of the blockade, no less enjoyable than Scarlett's. *There's the fourth.* Sharp features placed softly on a thin face, unassuming of the evil intents I found him capable of during the deep dive I did on the family. At first glance you would think Areus spent his time larping in the park, playing D&D in a dimmed basement, never having picked up a weight in his life, hot in a Sandman kind of way but no presence of strength. My eyes roll at his assumption of intimidation and restart my feet out the doors of the lobby to the busy sidewalk. I'm sure that the facts of his involvement in any crimes or violence he's been associated with have been based only on his presence during the acts as opposed to any actual participation.

I rub the soft triangled cat ears of my steering wheel cover, the vibrations in the car soothing my cells as the voice coming through the speakers washes over me. There is something calming about being in a small echoing space as the bass radiates through you like electricity, overstimulating in the best of ways. My shoulders shimmy as the cold liquid falls down my throat, the sun blinding my eyes from a clear view of my surroundings, the visor offering no assistance to my five-foot three frame. My driveway is a small opening in a fence of rose bushes surrounding what appears to be an exceptionally unspectacular brick colonial, the inside, however, is completely restructured. I had the entirety of the first floor gutted, not a single wall in sight, the second-floor half removed giving me a high vaulted ceiling and a large open loft, a sliding barn door barely hiding a walk-in closet.

I shift my ankles as I walk toward the tub, stepping out of my shoes, my socks, my jeans, and start the faucet. Letting the water run over my wrist I close the tub, setting my angled body on the edge of the of the large claw foot porcelain, I add dried rose petal and baking soda from the wooden board hoovering over the rising water. I remove the remaining articles of clothing from my chilled body, I must've forgotten to reset the auto temp before I left. I sigh in relief, in pleasure, emerging my aches into the warmth, the scent easing my thoughts, my hands roaming my skin in an attempt to wipe off any negative stimulation. I force myself to still, to simply sit and rest, to relax in the pleasing flush of warmth.

The ring of my phone wakes my mind from its rest. *Shit.* I forgot to call Jessyca when I woke up. I can already hear the frustration in her voice as she interrogates me on my actions from the night, I can't fault her though she did get me this job all those years ago, and handles my paperwork. I step from the tub, my nipples peaking at the surprise of the cold air, the water dripping from me in light splashes leaving footprints behind me as I walk through the kitchen and grab my phone from the counter. I run my fingertips over gritty iron, filing my skin as I make way up the twisting stairs, the unlit loft encasing me in shadow, waiting for the call back I know all too well is coming. I swipe the ring away, bring the phone to me ear. "Good morning" I sing out. "Don't be cute with me, try again" her words led by frustration "you know I hate having Time Bomb Timmy in my office". Timothy Clarke is a walking case of gastroesophageal reflux disease surrounded by the crinkle of antacid foil. I place the phone on speaker, resting it in between the two security monitors on the table in the middle of my closet, freeing my hands to pull clothing from the hangers over my moist body. "Love you too" I swoon with sarcastic endearment "I'm fine by the way". "Was that in question" she asks mockingly having full faith in my ability to have completed the task without difficulty. Laughing I swipe the phone off speaker, bringing her voice back to my ear. "Can you just run me the big three so I can turn in the damn report" I can hear the cringe in her voice at the idea of having to risk Timmy impatiently coming back into her office. "Clean pick up, clean scene, no witnesses" I submit to her request. "Thank you", the clacks of the keys sound rhythmically beneath her words "Marloe's, 6 o'clock?" she cues, more of a statement than a question. "Was that in question" I copy back with a sarcastic playfulness. "Bitch" she chuckles out, bringing us both to a full laugh. "Late or not at all" we agree in unison, I swear I could not have been gifted a better best friend from the universe if I had handpicked her qualities myself, our souls were meant to find to find one another. I toss the phone to the bed turning to the mirror, creasing my nose at the state of my hair, how is it I can have so little hair, yet it always remains a mystery to me what shape it should take for the day. I decide on the usual, straight and over to one side. Clipping all my hair to the top I brush the close fade of my wrapping undercut into a neatness and make my way from back to front with the flat iron. I open the drawer under the monitor, scrunching my nose at the foundation, skipping the mascara as well. I'm just going to clear coat my browns for shape today. I add a thin layer of eye shadow, lightly speckled with glittering flecks. I peek down at the large array of lip balm, nothing fancy, nothing colorful, I don't even think any of them are glossy, and choose a simple honey almond balm. I look to my perfumes. *Rose.* My go-to scent. I stare at the mirror, I've never been pleased with my reflection, there's nothing alluring about me, no want worthy features within my face, or body, just average, though I suppose I could always be worse off. I fill my cheeks with air, giving myself a complacent nod. *Good as it can be.* I rise, heading downstairs, the last few chapters of a book calling out to me from the coffee table, longing to be read, as I curl up the corner of the deep sectional sofa.

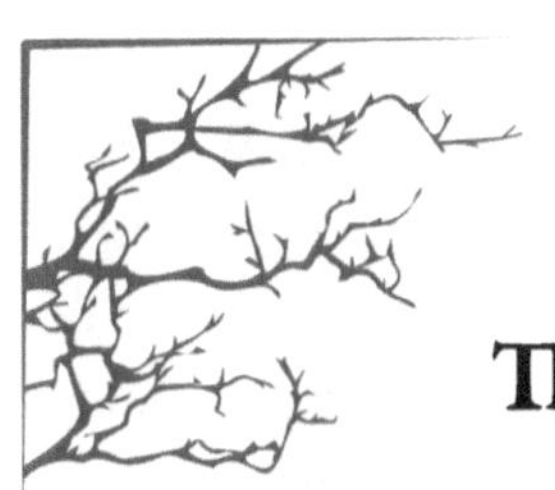

The Bodyguard

I can't keep my mind from wandering as I stare at the change of the little red bulbs, shifting into new numbers, the elevator lowering us down to the main floor. Why do hotels still bother skipping the thirteenth floor, like holding on to that old superstition actually makes the building safer. I guess most people really do just feel better having a belief system to hold onto, like the comfort they find in their belief of God. The ding of the elevator doors opening grab my mind back reality, shifting my body to move my feet forward. Stepping out into the lobby I glance left and right, quickly assessing the space for any sign of unwanted threat or attention, Connelly holding up his arm to be sure the doors stay open for us all. I take four steps forward, two to the side, giving room for the rest to exit behind me, pausing while the elevator doors shut. Connelly steps to my side, an ex-marine turned bodyguard dishonorably discharged after being scapegoated for the death of an innocent family, a mission his commanding officer went off book to accomplish. Followed by K, it's not her name but I know she isn't going be around long enough for it to matter, just another spoiled rich girl looking to piss off daddy by fucking the stereotypical bad boy with more money, more power, than anyone could ever need. Said bad boy, Ian Hayes, prince of the empire, basking in the warm glow of his father's reputation. Don't get me wrong I have seen firsthand the blood and dirt he is willing to get on his hands, but with us around there really is no need. Finally, we have The Boys, Scarlett and Silver, so named for Scarlett Witch and Silver Surfer, the comic book characters, they aren't twins, Scarlett seemingly Spanish, Silver looking quite Nordic. However, the two were found huddled together in a locked room during the raid of a drug den. By the doctors account both were about twelve, no record of having ever been enrolled in school and it appeared as if they couldn't read, neither even spoke a word for weeks. They were taken in by the Hayes family, like Connelly and I, together we flourished into the *well*-adjusted psychopaths the universe wanted us to be. Shifting my feet, I lead us two by two toward the doors, the noise of the lobby polluting us with unimportant chatter, clinking of glasses at the bar, and clacking of fancy shoes on the marble floor.

My ears perk at the voice to my left. "Ian Hayes, it's about his father" I immediately halt, glancing over my shoulder, throwing a silent question of expectancy to Ian. He narrowly shakes his head. I rest my gaze on the man at the front desk, fixing my unblinking eyes on him as my steps resonate toward him. "Can I help you" I question from his left, nodding ownership of the situation to ease the nerves of girl behind the desk. His head leads his body in a slow turn as he takes in the distrust flowing freely my stiffness. He pulls a card from his pocket, turning a quick gaze to his left, to Ian. "Detective Carlson" the sight of Ian triangled by bodyguards tickles his words. He brings his eyes to mine with an understanding that he isn't going to get to Ian the easy way unless he speaks to me first. "Tristan Hayes was found dead last night" his words hit me dryly like a sandstorm blowing against a building. "Where" the question falls out of my mouth like hot soup. "This really is a conversation I should be having with him" he ticks his head toward Ian "don't ya think" slapping me on the shoulder as if he is congratulating me for understanding a bad joke. I meet my eyes to Ian's, an annoyed growl rumbling my throat, nodding agreeance to detective dumbass without looking at him. I let my eyes bounce between the group, gently shaking my head, running my hand slightly down the front of jacket palm toward the floor attempting to signal a stand down to the group. I notice K watching my face, she untwines her arm from Ian's, taking two small steps back, unlike the others at least she has the common sense to access the situation. *Maybe I will learn her name.* I can feel the emotion rise in my face, it should be sadness for the loss of the man who pulled me in from the rain of abuse my father poured over me, it should be, but its anger. A questioning look is growing in Ian's eyes as I struggle to get the words out. "This is Detective Carlson" my resolved words in a weak stammer "he has news about your father" his hand outreached waiting to be met with a shake. "What" Ian spits ignoring the civil gesture, Carlson lowers his hand with a raise of both brows. "I'm sorry to inform you that your father was found dead last night at one of his *construction sites*" sarcasm drips from the word, I'm sure to emphasize the rumors that his sites are a front for money laundering. He isn't wrong in the least, creating building code issues that have to be restructured and rebuilt paid to other companies owned by Hayes as well is how the family funnels money through, still I'm annoyed by his judgmental tone. Ian steps forward signaling my body to shift in front of detective dick to avoid what I know would be a regrettable scene, chalk full of various charges and holding time Ian doesn't need right now, he is going to have damage control to attend to. I shift my focus sporadically, the feel of eyes discomforting my thoughts, someone is a little too interested. From my peripheral I notice a stillness, she is locked onto Scarlett, enthralled at the mere sight of them, it's cute really but this isn't the time. I step slightly into her view, my shoulder blocking the ratio of her view, her eyes quickly shifting to mine in a roll of annoyance as she walks toward the exit. *Unintimidated, I like that.* "When can we see him" Ian rushes out, bringing my attention back to importance, his hand to my shoulder, an attempt to pretend his sense of calmness. "I have some questions for you before we go any further on that topic" even I can sense there's a discomfort oozing from the detective's lips. Ian takes a step forward, his arms shifting me to step over, filling Carlson's space with his increasingly intense stature. It doesn't take but a breath for Carlson to cave to the weak intimidation. *What a puss.* If it really came down to danger I'd bet money he would cower immediately, play dead like a possum trying to avoid being attacked. "I've been instructed against allowing any viewings" he pauses looking toward the ground, taking in a deep breath. He finds a way to stiffen his stance, looking back to Ian "given the state of the body" he rolls out as if he may actually have remorse for what happened to Tristan. I can feel the shift of our auras, as if we are all of one cellular structure suddenly confronted with a sense of urgency. "The state of the body?" Ian questions through clenched teeth "what are you saying". "The deceased was put through a great deal of trauma, it's been decided, at present, that no one have access to the body" sensing the impending verbal assault lingering on Ian's tongue detective dipshit swarms out a question of Ian's whereabouts last night between eight and midnight, as if he woke this morning craving passive suicide. "What" the word spilling from Ian loudly, angry with the absolute disrespect that he could be asked such a repulsive question regarding his own father's death. I pull a smile across my face for the sake of the onlookers. "This isn't the place" I squeeze through the uncomfortable smile. Clearing his throat Ian juts his arms out giving his sleeves a slight tug, smoothing his suit vest, attempting to compose himself. Giving Carlson direct eye contact he states that he will be at the precinct in thirty minutes to address any questions on the matter. Carlson nods in agreement, turns his keys in his hand, shifting his legs toward the lobby door. Ian instructs Connelly to see that Sarah gets home safe. *Sarah. Sarah. Sarah.* I'll have to be sure to remember that as it seems like she might be smart enough to keep around for a while. Sarah nods at Connelly with understanding, stepping around Ian exiting the lobby on Connelly's heels.

The building is small, but all the units shoved loosely in the windows are still unable to decongest the summer heat smothering our flock as we step toward the front desk. Immediately agitated by the ungraceful voice of Carlson "Mr. Hayes, perfect timing" the words wet, full, like a large gulp of liquid is stuck in his throat prohibiting a swallow. A light flourish of anger at his casual, friendly demeanor, reminiscent of two high school acquaintances greeting one another at the twenty-year reunion. With my eyes locked on Detective Douche I tip my head toward Ian "Short and simple" I don't want Ian giving himself the chance to say something stupid. I can see an agreeable nod from the corner of my eye, false smiles pulling our faces at the uncomfortable closeness Carlson has found in front of us. "Feel free wait in the lobby gents... and lady" I can feel the ire from Scarlett attempting to burrow holes in his purposeful ignorance, it isn't that Scarlett has an outward dislike to being referred to as a woman, it's that he said it in such a way as to separate her from the masculinity in her nature as well as the group. My pupils dilate on him, the prey to my inner beast, licking at the sweet idea of his bloody tongue in my hand, the warm liquid cascading through my fingers. The change in his face advises me to his discomfort as he quickly raises his arm, suggestively ushering Ian down the hall "room three" no inflection in the words yet unease fills each step, like I said, nothing more than a scared possum feigning bravery.

Ian's face is furrowed as he steps from the room, silently walking toward us, simply nudging his head at us to leave. He rushes down the stair to the sidewalk, turning toward the side street where we parked the car, his hands riffling his pockets. He pauses, looking back at me "lighter" he commands with a snap of his fingers. "You know Connelly's the only one with a lighter, what happened in there?" he needs to tell us the truth so we know how to best handle the situation. "Fucking trauma, a car accident causes trauma. He was fucking tortured". "What!". "They skinned him alive" Ian throws the unlit cigarette to the ground. *Tortured, who the fuck would even dare.* "We're gonna find who did this, but we've got to get out here". Personal relationship to Tristan aside, after hearing the details, I'm impressed with the method, torture in itself is uncommon, but flaying, the skill, alone, needed makes it hard to come by. It's a shame to have to kill them.

The Accountant

The swirl of the variating aromas fills my nose, coffee, brandy, hot chocolate, whisky, the occasional frozen fruity something or other with a dumb fucking name. Marloe's is the only fusion bar in the area, two drink maximum on alcohol, *drinking with class not to get trashed* is her personal motto. Jessyca swirls the brown liquid around in her glass, rushing it down in one large gulp, her exhale scented harshly of butterscotch, her lips pulled in a smile, her eyes pinched shut, whilst my brows are raised in confusion of the two opposing sensations marrying. I'd question the purpose, but I know I'd get no answer, *just part of the process* she'd say, her process being two drinks at the office, two drinks at Marloe's, two drinks at home, and passing out while her boyfriend drones on about his day, no efforts of intimacy from either of them. At thirty-two we should be spellbound by great sex on a regular basis. Jessyca, I think, after eight years together, has simply gotten to the point in her relationship where they have become numb to each other's touch, complacent in the idea of putting it off for another day. I, on the other hand have been disappointed by every sexual encounter I've had, sadly not just the men but the women as well, always lacking something I can't quite put to words. "You good" the unsuccessful whisper yanks my thoughts back to the present. "Yea, just wandering" I roll my eyes playfully, the two of us giggling lightly. Her phone vibrates, the scrunch of her brows pushing my eyes to the caller ID, *No Caller ID*, a quick sigh of frustration to compose herself "Bradbury" her forced smile radiating from her voice. Not her real last name of course, her favorite author since I made her read Dandelion Wine in the sixth grade. "Where" her smile fades instantly, her eyes jetting to mine "We'll be right in". *We*. The urgency in her eyes might understated, they never call me into the office, given my free reign they like to keep me as confidential as possible. "We have a problem" she barks, rising from her chair she nods her head to the door insisting I follow.

Six bodies crowd her well sized office, making it difficult to creak in amongst them, Time Bomb Timmy being one of them, sulking in the corner like a scared intern. I'm directed to a large leather chair in the middle of the office by insistence lingering beneath a friendly tone, Jessyca places her hand on my shoulder, her words forcing their attentions to her. "Yea well, she's dead now" draws my focus to the man resting his arm on the bookshelf to my right. "What" I shout demandingly "How". They found her where I left Tristan, laying strangled beside his dried blood, their attempts to gather information have expectedly hindered, however, even I can't deny that the chances of her murder happening so soon after I killed Tristan is NOT a coincidence, I'd bet money she overlooked something as simple as deleting the email from her sent folder. "They can't trance anything to me, all my correspondences are encrypted past civilian capabilities" I assure them pressing confidence, not in my ability but in Jessyca's, she created the system we use to conduct communications, no one is better than her, that's literally what they pay her for. "I created the site myself" she attests, rightfully boasting her capabilities, light nods of agreement pacing the room. "Your cold until further notice, approved assignments only, NO new requests" his eye contact with me is unwavering, commanding urgency of my compliance. Shifting his eyes immediately to Jessyca "This better stay down" a long finger shooting a point to her. The men shift from the spots, their feet assuming dominance over the floor as they move through the door, Timmy giving a defeated look to Jessyca as he smoothly brushes past.

"You only used the site right" Jessyca moves around the desk before me, falling into her chair, dropping her head into her hands. I throw her a look of offense, she knows I wouldn't make a mistake like that "of course, she must've said something, done something" frustration at her possible actions filling the syllables. I grab the laptop from my messenger bag, sliding it to her across the desk, agreeing to keep the low profile commanded of me. The dry rub of the leather as I rise form the chair pulls her attention "let it be, don't do anything stupid" she requests of me, her stare searching my brain for agreement, "just" she lifts her gaze exasperatedly toward the ceiling "just don't hurt anyone". "Shadows only" I agree pulling the door opening, throwing myself from her office, a sense of determination guiding my steps.

In the last three weeks I've learned a lot, backgrounds, childhoods, favorite foods, number of tattoos, every move they've made since the moment I was told of Roisin's murder, the suspects really do lay only within the five of them. It seems I overestimated their sense of loyalty to the matriarch of the family, given how easily they rid her from the world, not even a funeral, they cremated her, never returning for the ashes. The crew have been spending a great deal of their time in the construction office, which if we are being accurate is just a small warehouse in the midst of a few acres of gravel, a good thirty minutes from the main road, and closed from public through way by a tall electrical fence. I can't follow them in there casually, forcing me to occasionally hack a satellite when I find need to keep track of the traffic at the site, there's a steady flow of men they bring in that never exit, well not alive at least. Of course I know this is the process of information extraction, but I find that I am overly curious of both their methods as well as what they have gathered so far. There is no question as to my ability to get into the building and remain unseen, being the shadow I promised to be, the question is when. The screen offers me the image of a two cars driving through the dust and gravel, heat signatures of each car showing a driver, a passenger, and a person of unknow condition per trunk, the addition of a third person in the back seat which must be Connelly. I close the laptop roughly, *tonight*, no more waiting. I pull the security box from the upper corner of my closet, four beeps popping the lid open, retrieving a gold ring, appearing flat on the top with unseen micro needles, poneratoxin, something the lab whipped up to model the effects of bullet ant venom, one punch and the effects begin within fifteen seconds, temporary paralysis and burning. I don't know how they make this stuff or why but I'm glad they do. Its non-lethal so worst case scenario at least I can promise Jessyca I didn't kill anyone.

The drive to the warehouse is longer than I thought it would be, I'm sure, though, it is just all the stop signs, given its use both on paper and in reality it needs to be out of reach. I could've cloned a key card for the gate, but I can't drive in without triggering the ground sensors. Luckily the satellite shows me there's a small shed just outside the fence among some decommissioned cement trucks, allowing me to drive here, and park inside, I can imagine that would be a very strange taxi rise, not to mention a paper trail.

I pull up my mask, thick to conceal the heat of my breaths from the chilled night air. Lugging the rubber sheet, I hope will serve to protect me against the fence, I jump onto one the cement trucks and climb to its highest point, tossing the rubber over the top of the fence like a blanket. I press my feet into the metal launching my body over the fence. *Fuuuck.* Tuck and roll my ass, I feel like I just reverse belly flopped onto a steel beam. I force down a groan, rolling onto my stomach, fists pushing against the ground barely succeeding at lifting my body up. I gather my composure, stretching my arms up behind me, shaking the pain from my shuffling legs.

I slide my body through the narrow opening of the door, eliminating the chance for the chilled metal to creak from my pull. I walk close to the wall as my eyes roam the darkness, searching for clues. I can see a small light across the open level, *an elevator.* No doubt I'd be discovered before the cage doors even opened, but, where there's an elevator there's stairs. I force my eyes to analyze every inch of my view. *Gotcha.* I still at the top of the stairs, pulling down my mask, listening for footsteps, voices, sounds of intention to the occurrences below. I keep my steps softly rushed, pretty sure there's no one at the bottom, best to get down and get hidden quickly. The light of this level is sharp, stealing the shadows almost entirely from behind the rows of shelving units, various tools and boxes stacked full to the ceiling. I rush out behind the last row of shelves, shifting my feet forward assuring the best position for both sight and sound. The two bodies from the trunks are alive and well for all intents and purposes, wrists tied to their chair arms, tape covering their mouths, each foot tied to its own chair leg. Ian is resting his ass on a metal table splayed with knives, Connelly standing stiffly behind him, arms crossed. Scarlett standing behind the man to the left, Silver behind the man the right, each of them with their hands dominating the men's shoulders. Areus stands in front of the men, a large dagger twirling in his hand. I hold in a laugh, of the five of them I find him to be the least intimidating, it wouldn't be a far venture to assume the two hostages feel the same. "You know the drill gentlemen, simple questions, simple answers" Areus stills his body, bringing his hands behind his back, the knife loosely in his fist, he nods at Scarlett and Silver, and they remove the tape from the men's mouths. The men flinch within themselves, the tape waxing hair from their chins. Areus steps to the man on the left, meeting his shin to the man's frozen knee, "What did Roisin pay you for". "Two crates of guns, no seri, ahhhh" the scream echoes the large room, a rattle of surprise jolting through me. Areus pulls the knife from his thigh slowly against his squealing groan "What would she need untraceable guns for, let alone two crates" he asks lifting the man's chin with the tip of the knife, his own blood trailing down his throat. "I.. I don't know" the whisper mumbling from his trembling lips. "What was that" Areus tips the knife the knife pressing the pointed end into his skin. "I don't know" the man yells out. Areus steps to the man on the right "What did Riosin pay *you* for "he accentuates the redirection of the question. "That's the truth, I, nnnaaah" the man gnarls against the quick blade. "I just don't think this is working" Areus again pulling the knife slowly from the man's thigh. A smile pulls my lips, realizing I was wrong about the cleanliness of his hands. Areus stiffens, his body enlarging his presence, his power, he raises his hand to his waist, palm up, jumping two fingers. Scarlett removes their hands from the shoulders of the man before them, a devil's smile pulling their lips, stepping around the front of the man, Scarlett's left leg planting between his, their right leg to his side. Areus makes a likewise move, his right leg strongly placed between the legs of the man before him, stomping his left leg down at the man's side. The two of them dominating a standing straddle above the men's thighs. Simultaneously the two of them open their suit jackets, their arms sliding from the falling sleeves, lifting their tucked shirts from the pants, unpinning the buttons with an intentional slowness. I drop my mask, covering my mouth with my hand. *They're not!* Their belts gently clink with the opening of the button the beneath, the pull of their zippers quietly blaring. The men turn their faces away at the sights before them. Areus grips at the man before him turning his head to take in the view of his fearful friend, his knifed hand reaches out to the man before Scarlett, the blade finding that soft spot under the chin, lifting the man's gaze to Scarlett's center. "Open" his voice deepened, the command flushing me with warmth, my eyes dilating at the occurrence before me. The man's eyes plead with Scarlett, silently begging for mercy. "Open" Areus ruffs out again, ignoring the man's sorrow, the tip of the knife pressing further into nook of his chin. The man accepts the command, his chin falling down upon the release of the knife from his skin, Scarlett brings their hand to the front of them wrapping their grip around a large purple phallus, slanting it upward to the lips of the man before them. His neck stiffens, his head trying to retreat, as Scarlett's free hand moves to the back of his neck, pressing his open mouth forward around the extension, their tongue gliding over their bottom lip in enjoyment of the man's rigid discomfort. Scarlett releases the back of the man's neck, slipping the length from his mouth, spit dribbling from his lips, face red with a lack of breath. Scarlett runs their hand through the man's hair, pulling their bottom lip in between their teeth, fingers settling on both sides of his head gripping the hair behind his ears. Areus dips the bloodied knife under Scarlett's stiffness, peeking it upward, "Suck" the words gravelly and wanting. Ian circles to the opposite side of the table, lowering himself to his seat, Connelly walking behind him to a seat of his own, grim smiles crooking both of their faces. Scarlett pulls the man's head forward, inhaling sharply at the sound of his first gag. "Come on man, stop this, we didn't know anything" the plea of mercy flow from the man before Areus. "Ssshhh" Areus pulls his arm in, running the knife over the man's lips, lowering the steel to his cheek once again pressing his face toward his friend, forcing him to watch. Scarlett's hands pulling, pushing against the man's gags, a shiver radiating through me with gurgle of his throat. Scarlett's jaw clenches, throwing a nod to Silver, who's still behind the man seated before Areus. Silver lifts a hand from the man's shoulder, gripping the top of his head by his hair, "Don't fight it" softly falls into the man's ear. With Areus' attentions still on Scarlett gagging breath from the man failing to wiggle free from the rough hold around his head, Silver pulls at the hair of the man in his hands, roughly tugging his neck back, sliding his open mouth onto Areus, his girth forcing the man's lips wide. Areus releases a surprised groan at the warmth of the unwilling mouth being forced around his shaft. Areus grabs at the back of the man's neck, allowing Silver to sneak the blade from his hand. Moans fill the room, Scarlett's sweet like smooth whisky, Areus' ruff like growls of a starved wolf, drawing a heat and wetness from my core. Their hips begin to jut forward, the men's hands gripping relentlessly at the chair arms, faces red, veins pressing against their foreheads, eyes pinched shut, fighting for air against the pain. Areus tips his head back, a hum rolling from his throat, Scarlet releasing little pants from the increase in the speed of their hips, the sight of Areus' pleasure edging them on. The view of Scarlett's length filling the man's mouth, leaking spit from the corners of his lips, pulling tears from his cemented eyes give Areus a new focus. A loud ruff jets from his chest, his hips matching Scarlett's speed, the man coughing around his depth. He places his thumbs on the man's eyes, lifting the lids, watching the brown iris' fight to roll to the back of his head. Silver releases the man before Areus, placing himself behind Scarlett, his body close, wrapping a hand around their stomach. Balancing Scarlett as he lifts her leg over the man, to stand between him, lacing his fingers in Scarlett's belt loops he lowers the navy fabric off their hips. Scarlett shifts, swaying gently, the pants falling from pointed toes, placing their foot softly on the man's thigh, grace intertwining the rough face fuck they are subjecting the man to. Silver presses his bulge against Scarlett, pulling his shirt open with no care for the garment, one hand coming to Scarlett's hip, the other releasing himself from the confines of his pants, his tongue runs over his bottom lip, his membrum hard, thick, shinning from the moisture at Scarlett's opening. I suck in my bottom lip, I should be turning away in disgust, fleeing in fear, instead I'm aching at the sight of them, my pussy weeping with want. Scarlett thrusts fully into the man, hitting the back of his throat, forcing his head back, sliding their tightness down Silvers length with the draw back, their moans pressing my teeth into my bottom lip. Silvers grip reddening the caramel skin on Scarlett's hip, pumping them up and down his shaft, Scarlett taking the full length of him. Scarlett places their hands on the man's shoulders, balancing between the two pleasures, the speed of Silvers thrusts whiplashing the man neck Scarlett's large cock, wrenching coughed spit from his protruding tongue, curved around the girth, failing in any effort to breath. Scarlett gasps at Silver's relentless pace, fast, hard, and fully penetrating. Scarlett's pleasure flowing down their leg as Silver grunts, his hand coming to the back of the chair, pulling himself past his depth into Scarlett, Areus groaning deep rumbles, the sight of them enhancing the pleasing throat fuck he is inflicting on the toe curled man before him. Scarlett's opening sucks tightly around Silver's veining throb, reaching around their nails dig into the back of his neck. A loud groan stifles within Silver's clenched jaw, white cream flowing from Scarlett's opening. Silver jerks himself free from the weeping hole, Scarlett's empty lungs gasping in air. Silver's fingers milk his cum from Scarlett as they grind against his hand, back arching, the large purple cock pressed firmly against the back of the man's throat, his body convulsing with the need for air. Areus' forceful thrusts slow, deepen, as he turns his head, taking in Scarlett's climax, his bottom lip pinched in his teeth. A grunt shift his glance back to the eyes his thumbs are forcing open, fully rolled to the back of the man's head, bloodshot veins bulging in desperation, cream dripping from the corner of the man's mouth. The three of them shift their glances amongst each other as the experience singes permanently into my memory. Silver pulls his fingers from Scarlett, the large purple shaft falling from the man's limp mouth. Areus hums, the man's mouth releasing his still hardened cock, his grip no longer holding the man's head upright. The men gasping for air brings my mind back to a sense of clarity, their mangled faces curled in pain, their chins covered in light red drool, one man struggling to cough up the emission Areus clogged in his throat. My tongue glides over my bottom lip at the warmth of my dripping walls spread over my panties. *What the fuck is wrong with you Alex.*

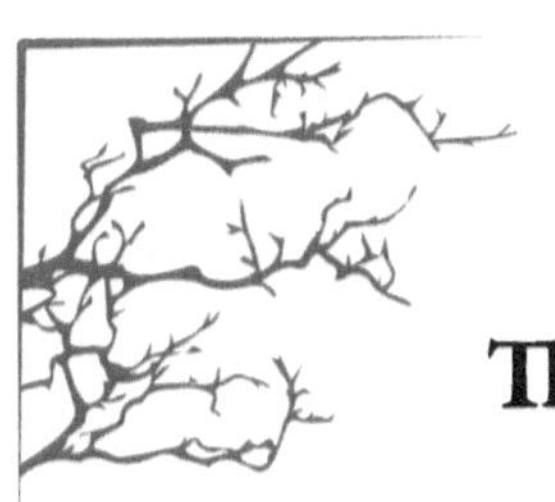

The Bodyguard

"Have we changed our tunes yet boys" I chuckle inn catching breath, my hands shaping my shirt into my pants, tightening my belt around my waist. From the corner of my eye I can see Scarlett, stepping back into their shoe as I brush my palm against the cotton donning my chest, swiping away the nonexistent wrinkles. "What did Roisin pay you for" Silver accompanies my words with the hilt of the knife falling back into my palm. The men cough at the pain of forming words "That's alright, I'll give you a moment" my gaze falling to Connelly, rising him to his feet. He slides a pipe off the table as his heavy steps carry him to my side, the pipe swinging a half circle in front of him into his other hand. "You said she paid you to deliver two crates of guns, serials wiped, now why would that cost a million" my knees bend my body, squatting low to the ground, the dagger dangling loosely by my feet. The man to my right croaks "three hundred thousand" the words burning his throat "she gave us three hundred thousand". My body shoots up, Ian rising in unison "What" his neck tight around the words. "She called a month ago, said she needed two crates of wiped guns, ammo to match" his voice breaks in a stutter, unable to swallow easily "said her husband was dying and she wanted her family to be ready for any push back". "I fucking knew it" Ian's fists crash on table. "We dropped the shipment at the Folton building. Connor. The guy's name was Connor". My eyes fix on Ian's as I step to the table in front of him, the light nod of his head giving me all I need. We can trust, at this point that he is telling us the truth, they still won't be walking out of here alive, but I can do them the curtesy of making it quick. I let the knife slip from my fingers gripping up the gun, twist my frame back toward the men, a shot to the head of each. "Whoo" Silver shouts above the smack of his palms meeting. "I want Connor here now" Ian grits. I bring my phone to my ear, informing Connor we have a cleanup at the warehouse that needs immediate attention. I relay Connor's estimated half hour arrival time to Ian, cutting the tape at the man's ankles and wrists, Scarlett mirroring my action with the other man as Connelly places tarps on the ground. Tipping the chairs forward we flop the bodies from the chairs, chains around their necks and ankles, two stabs to each lung. The Hayes theory is *if the lungs don't bloat the body don't float*, there's some flaws to the logic but it hasn't steered us wrong yet. We pull the plastic around the bodies for easy traveling, "Ready for the boat" I offer assurance to calm Ian's mind.

The elevator strains, lifting to the main floor, shifting our stances toward the rusted cage door as it returns. "I got the van backed up to the door" Connor points a thumb over his shoulder, the gate waiting to be pulled open as the elevator lowers to a halt. "Great. Cargo's over here" I invite him, his hand sliding the door, as he steps forward. He reaches down in an attempt to lift the body, interrupted by a swift strike from the pipe in Connelly's heavy hand. I slip my foot under his shoulder, rolling his body over, his hand cupping the gash on the back of his head. I place my foot on his chest, resting my arm loosely my bent knee "Why did you collect those guns for Roisin" I coo with a sarcastic tenderness. "I don't know wha" the words faltering to a wrench as my weight bares down on his cinching his chest, his ribs bending. "I ssswe" my balance shifting, increasing the weight against his lungs. "Okay" he forces out "okay" slapping my leg like he's quitting a wrestling match. I lean back, easing the weight smothering his body, his lungs rushing air in. "She wanted to be prepared for Tristan's death" his hands attempt to lift my foot from his chest "She didn't give me any details, she just said she'd take care of it". The anger of his response presses my heel to his chest, "I swear" the promise is lost on me, my body shifting its balance down on him, a scream echoing the room as his ribs crack beneath my weight. Ian places his palm on my chest, lifting my body off Connor, peering down at the traitorous snake. "What did she promise you" he asks gruffly. "Once y... you took your fathers sssseat" the pain stammers his words "I would take yours". Ian's eyes darken, his foot swiftly crashing into Connor's face, a small crack beneath the sole of his shoe, bringing his foot down again, and again, blood squirting from the ripping skin. Once more Ian brings his foot down, with another crack of bone, blood quickly coating the ground around Connors flattened skull. Ian growls through the revelation that Roisin didn't just have a hand in Tristan's death, she planned it, financed it. *Why would she be dumb enough to do this?* Ian wipes his foot across Connor's chest, disdain smearing the chunky blood from his shoe onto Connor's shirt. "Who do we have for this" frustrated annoyance riddles Ian's question, who *do* we have. We know Roisin made two five hundred-thousand-dollar payments, we know she wired them to a foreign bank account, what we don't know is who's, Connor was the one meant to hire a team that could trace the funds to the recipient. Scarlett drags the body onto a tarp, adding the chains around his neck and ankles. "What about Blake" uncertainty in my voice, crouching over Connor's body, delivering two knifed jabs to each lung, pulling the van keys from his pocket as I fling spit to his disfigurement. I stand to face Ian, Silver wrapping the tarp around the carcass. "About Blake" regret drips from his sung words. "You didn't". He meets my question with the pull of a crooked smile across his mouth. "How bad" normally I wouldn't care, but as it turns out we currently need her help. His tongue glides over his bottom lip, brow arching, "Shit" my eyes roll, one hand on my hip, the other attempting to rub away the throb behind my forehead. Ian has a rare tendency to leave his sexual conquests damaged, though he's usually smarter than to allow such a loss of control with one under his thumb or payroll. A quick huff shoots from my lungs "I'll find someone" a poor attempt at confidence wavering in my statement.

The air is cold as we exit the building, lowering the heat of frustration within me, brisk needles stinging my lungs, awakening the stifled skin beneath the layers of my suiting. A breeze fills my nostrils with the scent of stale gasoline, Connor left the fucking van running, *Dumb shit*. I pull the back doors open, Scarlett and Silver hoist the bodies sloppily into the small metal cave. I toss the keys to Silver, Scarlet closing the passenger door around her. "Slainte" I wish to them, my hand waving two lose fingers from my forehead, as they drive to the road. "Check on the bar , meet us at the marina" Ian instructs Connelly as I close the passenger door around him on my way past to the driver's seat. The immediate dryness blowing on my face as I sit shots a sharp look to Ian, "yea, yea" his annoyed hand lowering the strength of the air "fucking werewolf" he chuckles lightly. I give him a comedic howl of agreeance, my foot pressing the gas, gravel kicking up dust behind us, Ian howling harmoniously with me. Laughter gently busts from us, Ian nudging my shoulder with the loving pat of a brother. I harshly press down on the brake, shifting our bodies forward with the jut of the car, stopping suddenly, my eyes focusing on the fence in the side mirror. "What is it" confusion setting Ian's eyes on me. Reversing the car, Ian's head turns, eyes focused on the back window, my eyes focused on the incorrect visual in the side mirror. The car shifts to a stop, "Do you see that" I lower my window at the question, my eyes focused on a black object hanging over the fence, "What the Fuck is that" Ian asks opening his car door "is the fence on?". I open my door, grabbing up a few rocks as I step my body from the car. I toss the pebbles at the fence, the electricity sparks, demanding Ian to step back. I reach up and place my hand on the object "rubber" my eyes shifting toward the warehouse. "Carlson!" Ian tugs at the rubber angrily. Ringing pulls Ian's hand to his pocket, "not now" he barks into the phone "are you fucking kidding me... Connelly is on his way, I'll be right behind him" his growl of anger steaming the air "Carlson is at the bar, we've got to catch up to Connelly". "You go" I nod over my shoulder to the car. "What". "Someone's here, it's got to be handled" we both know I'm right. "Once I've delt with Carlson, I'll send Connelly to The Boys, and I'll come straight back here" his insistence promising as the car door closes him in. "Go, I got this" my palm hitting the roof of the car twice, forwarding it to the road, my focus steady on the gate to ensure its close.

Opening the door is almost painful, the grinding of the metal ringing in my ears, my eyes straining to take in the objects of the dark room. The whir of the elevator focuses my attention, I step to the side behind a wood piled pallet, my arm reached to light switch behind me. The elevator grunts to a settling, the cage door rattling open as a figure steps toward the middle of the room. I flip the switch, pausing a small woman in place, the breeze from the open door swaying the hair that's fallen her face to her chin, her frame is wide but well proportioned, skin caramel light like pale coffee. She knows she is seen, her eyes are searching for the impending presence, her body stiff yet calm, my brows low. It's her, Scarlett's little admirer. *What the fuck is she doing here.* Her body tenses, feet pressing against the floor, her legs carrying her steadily toward the door, as my eyes calculate her projection I extend my arm. Her throat hits my open palm, the force closing my fingertips around to the soft nape of her neck, a choke falling from her surprised lips, her hands dart tightly around my wrist. I step out from the shadow of the palate, forcing her steps back, my free hand shutting the door behind me, slamming her back into the uneven wall of two by fours on the palate. My eyes roam her face, chubby, but pleasant, flushed from the pressure of my hand. Her eyes surprised but not afraid, amber brown, light like well-lit stained glass. The scent of sweet roses pull my face forward, the tip of my nose meeting hers, her eyes are down, fixated on my closeness. She releases a grip from my wrist, shooting a fist toward my face, she's fast, but not fast enough. My hand matches her speed wrapping around her dainty wrist, pushing it into the wooden above her head, my fingers tightening around her neck. I force my thigh between her legs, lifting her from the ground. I'll be damned if I let this little bitch kick me. My eye contact is broken by the presence of her mouth, close enough to breathe in her surprised exhale, sweet and spicy, cinnamon and mint tingling my taste buds. "Who are you" my is vision shifting between her eyes and the fullness of her lips. Her body wiggles against my grip, but her eyes never change. "Drop it, you're no good at playing scared" I can feel a smile crook the corner of my lips. "I'm a cop" the words fight for freedom from her tight throat. I press my body into hers "Lie" my eyes taking in the changes of her face, her thoughts searching for a better pretends. I let my gaze wander to her collar bone, the neck of her shirt has slipped from her shoulder exposing thin black lines in the shape of a small minimalistic fox resting under a slim bra strap. *Adorable.* "Private" her struggling words call my eyes back to her lips "private investigator". Intrigue lifts my sights "And what did your investigation yield tonight". She fixes her eyes to mine sharply "everything" her shallow breath is heavy with accusation. I can't stop my eyes from eat the beauty of her fearlessness, "everything?" I play at her sarcastically with obvious disbelief, her current demeanor too calm to have bared witness to the interrogation. She clenches her teeth "every.thing", the feisty bravery in her unwavering eyes stiffen my cock against my zipper, "Well then" I swipe the tip of her nose with mine "what should I do with you now little fox". Her bottom lip curls between her teeth, pupils dilated, her thighs giving a gentle squeeze to my knee between them, my eyes lower to the warmth coming through her jeans. I raise a brow, my head cocking to side, the image of her alluring building a want in me. The wiggle of body refocuses my mind, lifting my eyes to hers, the shiny iris' struggling to look down. I twist my wrist dropping my hand from her throat, my palm turning around her arm, meeting her wrist to the other over her head, taking both her wrists in one hand. I slide a finger behind the button of her jeans "so easily caught for such a sly fox" I shift my weight, a slight distance between us, my fingertips guiding my palm down the smooth warmth of her skin, met by the silky band of her panties. Realization comes to her face, my eyes etching the look onto my memory, "Wait" her voice is small and quivering with no sense of demand. I slip my fingers past the fabric, creeping to her heat as she pinches her eyes shut, her lips curling inward with a discomforted hum. My jaw lowers dropping my mouth open as my fingertips sliding over her slick jewel to her puddled slit. She didn't just see everything, she liked it. Attempting to ward off my intrusion she clenches tightly at the swipe of my finger against her opening. Her nub stiffens beneath my fingertips as she gasps, my bulge jumping at her tight breath. Pulling my hand from her jeans, I rub my thumb against my middle finger, bringing my finger into my mouth, my tongue pulling the sweet warm liquid from my skin. She brings her sight down, watching my tongue smooth across my lightly parted lips. She's fucking delicious. I bring my palm to her cheek, gently smearing the moisture across her bottom lip, her dark pupils shifting between my eyes, the halting of her breath straining my length against its encasement. "Such a waste" I meet my mouth to hers, my words caressing her lips. I rest my forehead to hers, slipping my thumb from her lips, wrapping her throat with my hand. Her chin dips at the strength of my grip pressing her neck into the wood behind her head, her writhing body failing to free itself from my hold. My eyes are pulled to my hand by a burning sensation, *What the fuck.* Her hands jet to my wrist as my arm falls from above her head, a small red square imprinted in the crook between my pointer finger and thumb. A stiff numbness burns through my body, her fingers prying my hand from her throat as the distance between us grows. My back hits the ground, wisping saw dust around my faced. I feel her foot hit my ribs shifting my frame, pain should cinch my body but I don't move. She holds her throat and her stomach, coughing out the choke of her breaths, her inhale still heavy as she looms over me, her foot nudging my outstretched arm. Her head tilts to take in the angles of my carcass, her feet come to the outsides of my waist, legs bending her to a low squat as her ass grazes my hidden base. "It's a paralytic" she's fucking smiling at me, removing a golden ring from her finger "always comes in handy" her smug lips flame the anger in me as she throws the ring across the room. I try to speak, to yell, to threaten... nothing. She reaches down, straightening my collar, running her hands down the front of my suit, ridding me of creases. "Who's the little fox now" she coos dominantly, her eyes fixed to mine. She stands, her eyes lowering, *Fuck*, her foot pressing half circles into my dick like she's putting out a cigarette. She digs her foot, leveraging my shaft as a step off, her frame fading from my view. She's playing a dangerous game, I've got her in my scope now and I will catch her, break her, tame her.

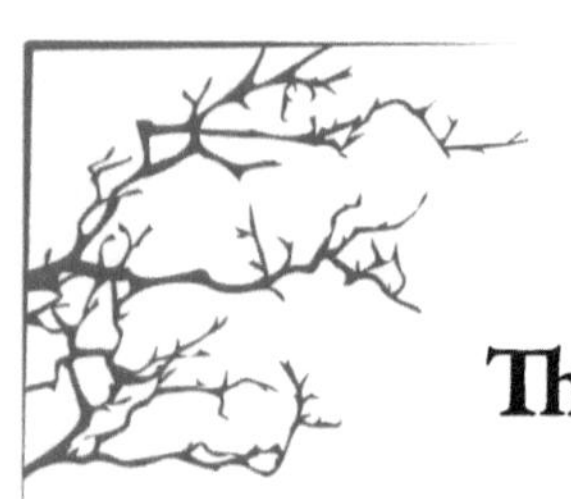

The Accountant

The gate comes into view quickly, no point in avoiding the sensors now, they already know someone was here. My arms pull the doors to the shed, my eyes searching the darkness for any lingering shapes or immediate threats. Starting the car, my movements jet into autopilot, rushing the vehicle to the road. *What the fuck, how do you get yourself into this shit.* I stop at the turn onto the main road, idling the car, my nose pulling in as much air as my lungs will allow, my warm exhale cloudy in the cold car. With no cat ears to distract my anxiety my grip on the steering wheel tightens, my feet planted against the floor mat, back merging into the seat. I close my eyes, searching for a silent spot in my mind, avoiding the replay of what I just saw, how it felt to watch, how it felt when he touched me, like a dying flame being kindled. My walls tighten at the memory of his beastly nature, his grunts reverberating the marrow of my bones. A sharp beam of a light pulls open my eyes, headlights rounding the corner past me. *Shit that must be Ian.* In the stagger of it all I didn't have a chance to consider the fact that Areus was alone at the warehouse, the toxin is short lived, he'll be resurrected by the time Ian gets to the building, uneasy on his feet, but walking none the less. I quickly shift the car into to drive, haste screeching the tires.

The Balling Beach Bash at the ocean front has the street flooded with movement, as I pull over into the loading zone in front of a bar, leaving the car running and immediately blending into the crowd. Thinking back I can't be sure whether the car was discovered or not, of course it doesn't help that I was parked so conspicuously at a yield sign in the middle of the night on the only road to their warehouse. The cops will quickly spot the unmanned car and they will flock to its conspicuity, eventually towing it from the street, and given the way I left Areus I know I need to deter them. The real danger lies in the fact that I let Areus get the drop on me as he is now intimately acquainted with my face, I'll have to truly keep it low key for a while. Luckily I've been able to pattern the basics to their daily tasks so I will be able to avoid them, especially seeing as how I don't need to watch them anymore. I've learned enough. They know Riosin not only authorized Tristan's death but financed it, they labeled and killed her so-called partner in the scheme, and as far as my role in this, Jessyca closed out the account the day I got put on desk duty, and no one they hire will be able to trace that account to me. It really is just a matter of keeping my face out of their way. I force my way through the bustle of the horde toward the familiar hotel that will be my home for the next couple of weeks. I just want to sleep and save the worry of Areus roaming around alive and well, with my face etched into his mind, for another day.

Aaaacchhh. The sun beams burn through my pinched eye lids, my arms and legs stretching as far from each other as my muscles will allow as I yawn out my detest of the unsubtle wake. My body shifts and rolls, hands patting in search of the vibration waking me. "Yeea" I croak gravelly. "I'm pulling up, we've got to go in" her tone perked with worry. "Why" I grunt out, sitting up. "They're catching up to you, Alex, an alert came through from IT this morning, they're searching for you with a fucking video still". *Fuck.*

I jump to my feet. "You went to that fucking warehouse didn't you?" her disappointment making me feel like a teenager brought home by the cops. The nagging truth that I'm not hard to find finally coming to fruition, no one can trace my fieldwork back to me, but it's not like I have a secret identity, with my picture it's not hard to find out where I work, where I live. The question is how long have they been flashing this picture over the internet, how much time do I have. "I need coff.." "girl get your ass in this car" she cuts in, I can hear her eyes rolling at the audacity of my statement, as if I don't know she already has a coffee for me. I trudge through the lobby, my limbs heavy, my mind foggy. I imagine this is what a hangover must feel like, well, with the addition of nausea. Luckily she pulled up right in front of the door. As I come through the passage onto the sidewalk she shakes an iced coffee at me to hurry into the car, impatience raising her brow, I shimmy my shoulders slowing my pace. The passenger window comes down "bitch get in" she chuckles, I smile widely at her, nodding in agreeance. My peripheral catches a still figure to my right, unease settling on the nape of my neck. *Areus*. He is standing ten feet from me, his hands sliding into his pockets, tongue rolling over his bottom lip, a smug smile widening across his face as his eyes burrow into me. He gives a slight nod, tipping his nose to the road, my eyes turn, following the invisible lead with urgency. Fear pulls my lips apart, my jaw falling to the ground. Ian is stepping toward the car. "JESSYCA" I scream, the happiness falls from her face, turning her attention to her window, Ian's arm swaying from behind him, the black cask releasing two bullets through the glass. "NOOOO" I fold into myself, my scream flowing through the air around me like a frozen breeze. A hand pulls my throat with a sharp burn, another at my waist, Ian waving at me through the distance. My legs weaken beneath me, the hand at my waist balancing my loose steps, lit police cars pulling to the scene. I scream with every burning cell in my being, "HEEELLP" the muzzled words barely releasing a gasp. The hand around my throat falls, scooping the backs of my knees, my body falling into the cradle of Areus' body, my head hanging back watching the police dim wittingly attempt to shield Jessyca's body from onlookers by covering the windows with jackets from their cars.

He lowers my folded frame into the front seat of his car, turning my flopped head toward him, "Look familiar" he pulls the ring from his finger, holding the band carefully between our eyes. *You've got to be fucking kidding me.* "Took me quite a while to find this but I knew it would *come in handy*" the corner of his mouth crooks to a half smile as he mocks my words back to me. He opens the glove compartment dropping the ring by a small gun and pulls out a roll of tape. He wraps the tape around my wrists and ankles as drops of sorrow past my control spill from my eyes. Closing the tape back in the glove box, he turns his vision to me, he eyes embracing the trails on my cheeks. He brings up a closed hand, raising my chin as he gently swipes at the moisture. An unexpected sensitivity flickers in his eyes "you brought this on yourself little fox, but I am sorry about your friend" his thumb caresses my cheek "now, I'm going to trust you can control your mouth when this shit wears off" he rises and closes the door, coming around the car into the seat beside me "what is the fuck is it anyways" he looks over at me "we'll save that for later" he chuckles to himself, shifting the car forward. The burning finally begins to fade, but I don't want him to know I'm gaining my faculties back, on the other hand I can't pretend for long, he knows firsthand that the toxin only last about fifteen minutes. "How you feelin" he questions as if he can read my mind, his eyes fixed on the road, "it's been like twenty minutes, I know you're good by now" he points to the time on the console. I peer at him from the corner of my eye, his overly casual demeanor invoking my ire. *Is he fucking serious?* "How do you think" I rasp, lifting my hands slightly at the annoyance of my capture. "We've got quite a drive ahead of us, are you ready to tell me who you really are" his eyes glancing out over the road, it's like he's actively avoiding my face. "Does it matter" I offer, sadness still lingering in my voice "where are we going". "Does it matter" he copies, sarcasm echoing in his retort, a quick glance at my face pulls a clearing from his throat, "my cabin" he states flatly. I shift my stiff body in the seat trying to wish away the tingle left behind from the muscle tightness forced by the toxin, my legs fighting against the tape, lungs too full of nerves to take in air as my gasps echo the car. His hand grips my thigh demanding my attention "I need you to breathe" his eyes now pinned on me, the shock of his worry halting my breath entirely. The car snaps my body forward, stopping in the middle of road as if it hit an invisible barrier. He brings his hand to my chest, warming the skin over my heart, breathing in through his nose with a nod of instruction, and out through his mouth, my lungs still frozen in confusion. "Alexandra" his voice rings me back to reality "breathe" he insists once again inhaling through his nose, I respire unsteadily as the burn in my chest begs me to follow his instruction. "Slowly" he instructs with distressed brows, my lids pinch tightly with disbelief of his fret over my wellbeing. Why would he care. "You're okay" his affirmation jetting my eyes open, the air flowing from his parting lips reminding me to exhale, "you're okay" this time his whisper almost seems grateful. "You know my name" the statement demanding further information. "I know everything about you". "Everything" I mock snarling my lips.

"Everything" his cheeks raise to a wide devilish grin, the memory of the flipped conversation between us at the warehouse rolling my eyes, "did you think you were in that hotel room alone?" the steadiness of his voice removing any doubt about his truthfulness from my mind. "You have a camera in my room?" self-directed surprise flooding my voice, how did I not notice that. "Yes, but..." his tongue glides across his lower lip "you know for someone who kills for a living you really don't pay attention to your surroundings do you" his bottom lip curls into his teeth. "I would have noticed if people were in" the shake of his head cuts my words, "not people darlin'. Me" there's a hint of assurance in his voice as if knowing he was the only one secretly invading my space would ease me. "Is that supposed to make me feel better" my body shifts at the discomfort, his eyes glancing over my movement through creased corners, no intention of responding to my sarcasm, "well you can't have been watching long, you only just triggered the search alert this morning". My arrogance is cut short by his laughter "you really underestimate me little fox" the byname flushes a low heat to my cheeks "did you think that little show for the cops would deter me after what you did" his grip tightening around the steering wheel, a yawning creak echoing from the leather, "what is that anyways" his eyes still shifting over the scene passing us. "If you already know who I am why did you ask" I question smugly. "I wanted to hear you say it" his voice flat and definitive "now, what is that shit". "Poneratoxin" I twist my wrists against the tape "derived from bullet ants, non-lethal, unfortunately" he hums at the insult, amused by my ill intentions. I raise my back from the seat of the car, stiffening my resolve "Why did you kill Jessyca?", his shoulders press back into the seat as he clears his throat, "That wasn't meant to happen" his hand wipes anxiety from his mouth "we were meant to take the two of you to the warehouse, but Ian," a pause lightly shakes his head "Ian has a tendency to let anger get the best of him" his huff is questionable, it almost seems as if he disappointed in his brotherly boss. I replay his words in my mind, I need to be sure I process all the information correctly, *wait*, "warehouse?" I whisper to myself "I thought you said we were going to a cabin?" my question tainted by my distrust of the situation, heightened by the lack of response from him. I've always known I would die relatively young, almost welcomed it, but something about dying at his hands pisses me off. I sigh, falling back into my seat, it's pointless to ask him where we are actually going or what he plans to do with me. Gazing out the window, my eyes blur at the speed of the scenery passing by, auto focusing until they close.

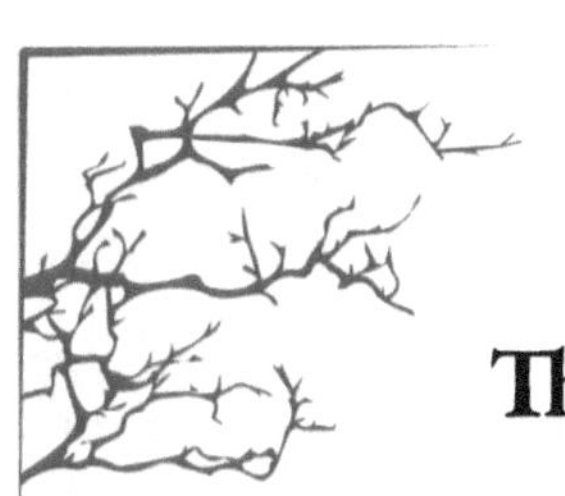

The Bodyguard

I lift the vibrating phone from the cup holder, surprised that it took Ian so long call. "Where the fuck are you" his voice loud before I can offer an acknowledgement of who even is calling. "I'm waiting near the marina" false confidence weighing down my tongue. "Bullshit. Is this about that bitch in the car". "We agreed it wasn't necessary" there's a control in my words as I attempt to keep my voice low. "This little crush of yours is clouding your fucking brain, they don't get to live" I can hear his jaw clenching around the gritty words. "You know what he did now brother. He fucked up, but it ended with your mother" reason lingers in my voice, hoping he will find a way to come to his senses. We can't ignore the assaults we learned of while watching Alexandra, Riosin had sent her quite a few pictures with the witness statements. It made me want to kill Tristan myself, I never would have thought the man that pulled me from my own sexual abuse would be returning that pain to the world. "Stand by your family *brother*" a sudden disbelief accentuating the word "it ends with her" my silence screams between us, my eyes shifting to her, the peaceful calm of her slumber washing over the anger of his plans. In the weeks I've been watching her, tracking her life, I have come to know all there is to her, her trauma, her fears and nightmares, her hopes and dreams, the goals she once had as a child. Her mother died when she was four, her father abused her both mentally and physically, trading her to other men for whatever worthless need he had at that given moment. At ten she befriended Jessyca, who had been similarly scarred by her own father as well, through the pain the two became sisters, like Ian and I became brothers. When she was sixteen their fathers were "killed by a bear" during a camping trip with the girls. Jessyca's aunt took the girls in, surrounded them with protection, made sure they were taught by the best fighters her money could buy in various arts, so they would never be vulnerable again. I think she may be the one person they were honest with. At twenty she joined Jessyca at ArcStone, a private security agency, no doubt due to the four deaths that surrounded her at that point, all mysterious but nothing could be proven. She is beautifully broken, damaged to perfection as if she was split from my very soul. I turn my eyes back to the road, "She isn't yours to kill" the finality in my voice immediately pulls a mocking laugh from him "she isn't yours to protect" the comedy fades from his voice "you *will* bring her to me". "She *is* mine" I lower my window, the rush of the cool air hardening my resolve "her death is mine to decide" I pull the phone from my ear dropping it out the window to the passing pavement. No matter how much I think back, no matter how many different views I gain of the situation I can't see where it happened, I can't find the moment she stopped being a target and instead became the object of my desire. Its more than a want I have for her, it's a need, not a need to fix her, I already accept her for all she is and all she can never be, it's a need to hold all the broken pieces and keep her from losing sight of them. Her body tries to fold into itself, *she's cold*, I raise the window removing the breeze from within the car. I can see the shadowed sign for Carlos' Café passing on the right, which means we are only an hour from the cabin. The cabin is relatively well hidden, only partially visible from the road, down a long dirt driveway surrounded by trees in a very ominous tone. I bought it about five years ago, cash of course, but never changed the title. I politely convinced the sellers to keep it in their name at double the asking price, an offer that were happy to accept. Ian doesn't know about the cabin, no one does, but that last call is traceable to only an hour away which is far too close for the cabin to be a permanent solution for her safety.

I pull into the garage, the light reflecting off the white walls, I rush my hand to the headlight switch, as not to disturb her just yet. I open her car door slowly, afraid she might somehow fall out, my eyes gliding over her slumbering frame. In the time I've been watching her she's made faces at her reflection, hidden her body from even herself, pinched and pulled at the things she would fix, it amazes me that she can't see how beautiful she is. Fit frame, athletic, trim but not slender, soft facial features placed evenly on her oval face. I'll admit she is average in many senses of the word, her chin length purple hair being the most attention-grabbing part of her, but she is beautiful none the less. I bend down, softly lifting her from the seat, I kick the door shut behind me, her head lifting toward my neck. "Why don't you just kill me?" she whispers up at me, sadness holding her eyes closed. Had anyone else said that to me I would simply laugh at the attempt to gain mercy, but I can only muster the urge to calm her, the foreign feeling offering her a simple "hush" as I carry her into the bedroom. I set her down on the edge of the bed, and she takes in the surroundings of dark wood and leather. I think the old tenets were going for an English smoking-room aesthetic. I turn, walking to the chair behind me, removing my suit vest. "Just kill me, what are you waiting for" defeat riddles her words, she truly doesn't understand, I can't expect her to, yet I can feel confusion raising my brows, my body turning to face her, "my death is yours to decide" she copies to me, her breath sticking the words to her throat as her eyes glaze. *Adorable.* I can't help but chuckle at how cute she is to think she is so powerless as I approach her, my hand lifting her chin, silently begging her eyes to meet mine, "you misunderstand". Thoughts shift across her face, the questions filling her eyes. "Your death is mine, little fox, because *you* are mine, mine to harm, mine to protect".

"What if I don't want your protection?"

"You will have it regardless".

"And what of your harm, who's to protect me from you"

My hand falls from her chin, reaching into the nightstand retrieving the switchblade, I flick the knife open as my body lowers to a knee before her. I cut the tape from her ankles, offering her a moment of my submission in exchange for her trust. I cut the tape from her wrists, lifting my eyes towards hers, "any harm you receive from me will be at the thralls of your pleasure" I turn the knife, placing the hilt in her hand, she needs to realize she never lost any power over me. Her eyes fix on the knife, I can see the all the ways she'd kill me swirling in her mind. "Why" her question almost confuses me, I have to remind myself that she doesn't understand our mirrored souls, "you and I are the same, made from grit and dirt and filth".

"So, you think what, exactly, we can fix each other?"

"I don't want to fix you, I simply want to hold you while we fall apart"

Her eyes soften and lift, roaming my face for a tell of insincerity, there isn't one, I mean every word and she can feel it somewhere deep within her. I keep my eyes forward as her body raises form the bed, part of me expecting a fight from her, instead her hand lowers, extended for me to take. She pulls up as I take it, raising me from my knee, "You know the game, simple questions, simple answers". It's cute how she thinks she can use my own words against me, nevertheless I yield to her with a nod. "Truth, you knew he was going to kill Jessyca, yes or no?" she locks her eyes onto mine, my hand still tightly within her grasp. "No" I speak finality into the word. "You know why I killed Tristan, yes or no?". "Yes" my chin dips in a slight nod of agreeance to her actions. "I am *safe* with you, yes or no?" the question ignites a hope, hope that she sees a possible future where I am not a capture, not a threat, but a sense of trust in her life. I twist my hand around hers, placing her palm on my chest, "Always". I bring my free hand to her face, caressing her cheek with my thumb, "always" I repeat, emphasizing the severity of my intentions. Our futures are forever linked. She turns, lowering her body onto the bed, shifting to the middle, pulling the pillow down beneath her head, her fear eased but her sadness prominently displayed. I shuffle into the bed behind her loosely, one arm sliding under her neck, the other draping over her as I take her hand in mine. She scoots back, molding her body against me, her round ass pressing against my growing length. Her hips shift rolling half circles across girth, my bottom lip curls into my teeth, she has to know what she's doing. "You should stop" it's not often I try to be gentlemanly, but she's been through a lot today. She turns her wrists, cupping my palm against her perked nipple "distract me" my cock jumps at her soft coo. "Careful little fox, my will is only so strong when tested". "Little fox? Am I your prey?" there's a rasp to her voice I haven't heard before vibrating at my core, pulling a groan of agreeance from my throat, "Then hunt me" the sudden demand in tone hardens my length, bulging behind her grinding ass, begging to be inside her. Her head jerks at the grip of my hand around her throat, pulling her head back, twisting my other hand from her grip, unbuttoning her pants and shedding them down her thighs. Her legs shift and kick, removing the pants fully from her legs, gasping as I pull at the band of her panties, ripping them from her body, tossing them into the void of the room. I lift her thigh back, draping it over mine, my fingers run the length of her leg, her supple skin tensing beneath my touch. I place my palm on her pelvis, hovering my fingertips over her gem, lingering in the warmth of her desire. "Please" her whispered plea exploding deep inside me. I slide my fingers over her nub, tipping into her wet opening, a hum rolling her tongue across her bottom lip. "Please" she begs again, her hips shifting her slit over my fingers. I press my bulge against her ass through the confines of my pants, as she continues to grind her opening over my fingers, edging her own pleasure. She closes her eyes lightly, her hand reaching around my lower back, increasing the pace I press into her. I curl my finger, slipping inside her as she grinds forward, her tight heat enveloping my finger. I pull my finger from her, circling her warmth over her button, the sound of her light moans tempting my imagination. I remind myself to be gentle, she needs care right now, I'll break her soon enough. In one steady move I shift my body, rolling her forward onto her stomach, my legs between hers, spreading her thighs apart. I place a hand on the back of her neck for leverage, steadying my knees for balance, two fingers circling her wet slit. I bring my fingers to my lips, my tongue falling from my mouth, licking the juice she's gifted me, groaning at the sweetness. If she wants a distraction, I'll give her one. I run my hand down her back, over her lifted ass, down to her begging center. I thrust two fingers inside, surprise muffling from her hidden face. I slide my fingers back and forth keeping pace with her breathing, quick but steady, her growing moans stifled by the pillow beneath her face. I release her neck, grabbing her hair, turning her head to the side, I need to hear her. Her gapping mouth sends electricity through my steeled cock. God, I want to feel the back of throat, I want to pull tears from her eyes and drool from her lips. I release her hair, raising myself back, the sight of her writhing body filing me with ache. I pull my fingers from her, one hand reaching under her stomach, the other gripping her thigh, rolling her onto her back, stretching her legs around my body. I slide two fingers inside her without grace, stiffening my wrist against the pressure of her tight walls. Her hands come down, her short arms attempting to press against my thighs, fuck she's cute when she struggles. I bring my left hand to her pelvis, rubbing my thumb over her swell, slowing the speed of my thrusts but increasing the power, a loud moan pulls her hand to her mouth. I've never wanted a scream more. I release her clit through a lightly pulled pinch, increasing the strength in wrist, as I reach up and pull her hand from her mouth, she bites her lower lip in a clenched jaw, forcing silence. I place her arm over her head, leaning against her wrist, coming face to face with her, "scream Alexandra, scream for me" her head presses back at the whisper, exposing her neck to me. I'll have to drive it out of her. I lift her hand, wrapping her grip around an iron rod of the headboard, rising my body from hers as I bring my thumb back to her pearl. She shifts her face into the nook of her elbow to dim her moans, and anger rushes through me. Shifting my legs back I bring my mouth down on her, sucking her jewel between my lips, my tongue rolling waves, my throat growls at the sound of her gasp. The scent of her sweet pleasure swirls my senses, her decadent flavor bewitching my tongue. Her feet slide against the silk sheets, her ass lifting off the bed, attempting to pull herself from me. My hand slides under her leg, gripping her thigh "Don't move Darlin" I pull her down, sucking her swell back into my mouth my tongue circling the tumescence. Her hand grips my hair so tightly I have to stiffen my neck against her pull. I release her from my suction, my tongue wide, licking up the essence dripping from her clench, "Fuck" my throat rumbles out a growl at the candied liquid. Her body tightens, her leg stiffly trying to wrap around my shoulder, her breath halted, lips curled into her teeth pressed to close together for air to enter. "Stop holding back Alexandra" her head turns back the crook of her arm, her lips pull from her teeth, her responsive gasp begging precum from my painfully hard cock, "scream" my lips glide the whisper over her gem. I suck her back into my mouth, the power of my arm thrusting my fingers forcefully through the pressure of her tightened walls, my grip falls from her thigh as I my reach around her pelvis, my thumb rubbing circles over her button peaking from the pull of my lips. Her moan finally releases, loudly reverberating against the grip of her hand in my hair. The arm above her head pushing against her tight grip around the iron rod, her core pressing into my face, my breath is hard to find, my ears greedy for her screams echoing in the empty room. "Stop" she shivers out a request I ignore, I curl my fingers slightly gaining access to her sweet spot "fuck, st...stop" she stammers loudly. Her hands fall from my hair, from the headboard, gripping the sheets at the arch of her back, my tongue sliding from the pressure of my mouth, drawing the weeping juice to my throat. I want to swallow every drop of her. Her legs shake around my shoulders, my fingers giving no relief of mercy to her climax, my groans vibrating her center, her orgasm falling to bed. Her legs fall to my sides, the tension in her body loosened, her fingers stretched out, palms lightly pressing into the bedding. I release her from my mouth, pressing my fist into the firm mattress, my fingers keeping their pace within her, coming to my knees. "Beautiful" my wide pupils burn the vision into my mind, her breath quickening through her stiffening body, a second wave rolling through her core, her legs close around my arm, her body rolling to her side, her hands reaching for my wrist as her pleasure moans through the air. Her grip traveling up my arm, lifting her back off the bed. I grab her hair supporting her limp frame, tipping her head back bringing her face to mine, pressing my cheek to hers, my ear to her lips, growling at the ache for her moans filling my ears. Her hand comes to the nape of my neck grasping at my hair, her moans becoming fast paced panting, "Cum for me" I order, deep and demanding. Her gasping mouth meets the nook of my neck, sinking her teeth into my skin, my clenching jaw sharply pulls air between my teeth, *Fuck. Go easy. She needs affection right now.* I have to force myself not to throw her body back and fuck her into a numb darkness. "Cum for me little fox", a moan pulls her teeth from neck, "I'm" her bottom lip caressing my ear "I'm cu" a deep gasp stopping her lungs, her body shaking in my hands. I still my arm, lingering my fingers within her throbbing grind, her lungs finding air. She pulls my wrist, slipping my fingers from her puddling slit, lifting my hand to her mouth, her tongue meeting my wrist. She licks up my fingers, closing her lips around her flavor. I can't hold back the growl raised in my throat, pulling my fingers from mouth with a pop at the pressure of her sucking her drippings from me. I lick her bottom lip, pulling it between my teeth, her lungs sharply rush in air at the surprise. She presses her hand against my chest, her head pulling back, meeting our gazes, taking in the curves of one another's faces. "You held back for me, yes or no?" the softness of her voice blankets sensitivity over me, "yes" I tap the tip of her nose with mine. Her hands come to the sides of my neck, her thumb guiding my chin toward her, she kisses me softly, her tongue rolling slowly around mine, her sweet taste still lingering between us, she bites my tongue as she releases me from the kiss, leaving her lips brushing across mine "don't" her whispered command floods my lungs.

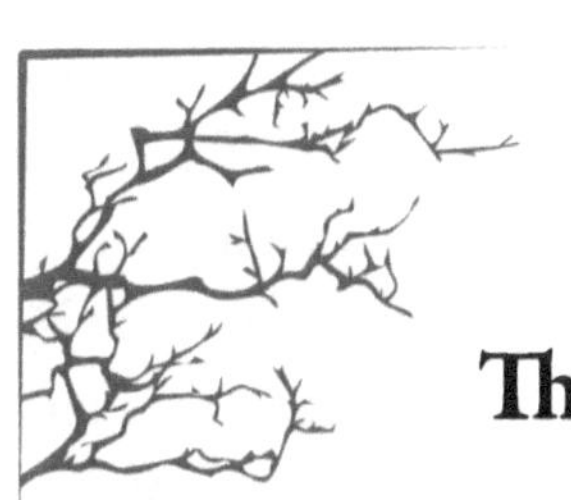

The Accountant

Knowing he held back to cater to my current emotional state fills me with a strange affection for him, I know I shouldn't feel this, Jessyca would kill me herself, but he is right, there is a commonality between us. I press my hand against his chest, walking him backwards off the bed with my knees, my hands undoing the restrictions around his fully visible length. I pull at the band around his waist, the well-tailored pants dropping to his ankles revealing his bare lifted erection. I drop to my elbow, placing a hand around his girth, guiding his tip into my wide mouth. He sucks air between his teeth, jaw stiff, the affirmation of his pleasure sends a new wave of longing through my core. I lower my lips down his shaft, my eyes pinching as he fills my mouth, my throat tightening around his tip in a gag. "Fuck" the whisper shocks my stimulated pearl. He pulls himself from my mouth, my neck drooping at the relief, taking a heavy inhale into my lungs. "You're not ready" he consoles, his hand patting my head. I grab his hand from hair, rising to my knees, mustering any sense of command I might have "I'm not some broken thing" the words crook a smirk from his lips. "Is that so" his mocking brows stir an anger in me. I am tough in a lot of ways, but I've seen what his capable of and he is right I'm not ready, but there's a stubbornness growing in me at the audacity of his weak vision of me. "Any harm I should feel will be at the thralls of my pleasure" I throw his words back in his face, the smile fading from his lips, unamused by my sarcasm. I bring my lips as close to his as I can, his height keeping me at a distance, "be careful little fox" his finger sweeps my hair from my face, I shift my head inviting his eyes to fix on mine, intensity brightening his green iris'. "Harm me" I plead, dare filling my whisper, the devil within him quickly taking over as a growl rolls in his throat. His hand jumps to my hair, pulling my neck down to the edge of the bed, his grip supporting my head as his cock forces my mouth wide. My eyes pinch at the assault to the back of my throat, his thrusts blocking air from my lungs as I cough against him. He pulls himself from my mouth, my lungs already greedy for air, he allows me two inhales, before shoving his full length down my throat again, a gag tightens my throat. "Fuck baby" he groans as a I cough out spit again him. He pulls himself from me, his thumb gently wipes at the spit sealing my eye. His hand comes from my hair, pressing my shoulders into the bed, repositioning my head to rest on the edge. He leans his knees to the bed around my head, his full spheres resting on my lips as his fingers dance circles around my sensitive nub. A moan parts my lips, his balls falling onto my tongue, I suck in swirling the sensitive rounds with my tongue. He blows air from his lungs, an unformed word hiding in the breath. My moans hum around the suckle of the soft skin in my mouth, "ahhh" he groans quietly pulling away from me. He allows me only one breath, before thrusting his full depth between my lips, my hands press against the motion of his thighs, my climax building against his hand between my legs. My moans clench my throat, gagging, coughing at the fill of him. He glides his length from my throat shifting my voice box as he passes, pulling his hand from my pooling slit, licking my surrender from his fingers. He wipes at my face, flinging the spit and tears to the floor. "Look at me" he growls, pinching the stray hairs from my eye lashes, his hand gliding the length of stiffness, "Give me your tongue" his tip rubbing my lips. I pull my lips apart, widening out my tongue toward my chin, the tip of his cock offering a small drip of pleasure to my taste buds, the warmth of my exhale on his veining shaft pull a groan from his lips. Instantly he is in my mouth, gripping my neck, squeezing my throat tightly around his girth, my arms pressing against the power of his thighs. "Fuck" he grunts pounding a cough from the back of my throat "that's it baby, you're doing so well" the praise electrifies my core, my nails dig into the soft flesh of his thigh, a heavy growl rumbling in his clenched jaw. "Fuck Alexandra" the pull back of his thrusts shorten, pounding against my gagging wretches, his throbbing cock lingering so deeply that his sweet cream slides easily into my stomach. He loosens the hand around my neck, placing is thumb on my chin, pulling his sloppy cock from my mouth. Sliding into my throat again, he shifts his hand from my chin to the back of my head, caressing my cheek on the way, pulling air between his teeth sharply as he lets his relaxed cock fall from my lips. I spit out the lingering emission my wounded throat is unable to swallow as I gasp for air.

He lifts my back up from the bed by the support of his hand gripped in my hair, his free hand gripping my legs, spinning my waist and me pulling toward him. My eyes are clouded but open, my hands gripping the sheet. He pulls his shirt apart, dropping it from his shoulders, his hand bringing the tattered cloth to my face, clearing away the mess of his pleasure. He pulls my legs around his waist, one hand lifting my ass from the bed, his other hand rubbing the back of my head, resting my face in the nook of his neck, cedar swirling within my nose, as his body gliding out of his pants and shoes. His weight shifts as he steps into the large tub, his hand coming away from my wet ass reaching for the faucet handle, his other hand supporting my neck as he leans me back. The warmth of the water rises around us as he grazes his fingers up my ribs lifting my shirt over my head, my arms rising to the ceiling weakly. Softly he runs his fingers through my hair, brushing it off my face as he lowers his hands to the clasp of my bra, unpinning it, sliding it forward from my arms and dropping it beside the tub next to my shirt. The crash of the water halts as he wipes my body with a soapy sponge, filled with the same aromatic woody scent my nose pulled from his neck. "Close your eyes Love" his voice now undemandingly soft as his forefinger lifts my chin, tipping my head back into the flow of the warm water falling from the sponge. "One more" his fingers run through my hair like a comb under the warm water from the sponge above my head. The sponge splashes into the water, his thumbs wiping my eyes dry. "I wish this was real" I chuckle, my forehead falling to his chest.

"why is it not" he rests his chin on the back of my head "how long did you watch, how much history did you gather?".

"what?"

"you didn't just walk into that warehouse void of information, how long did you watch me, how far back into my past did you gather your information from"

"not long" philosophically this isn't quite a lie.

"the truth, little fox" demand returns to his voice.

"three weeks before the warehouse", what is his point, is it a point he's trying to prove to me or to himself.

"*and*...two weeks after the warehouse, the same two weeks I was watching you. With every file from every therapist, psychologist, and doctor you've ever seen" his tone smooth and definitive as if he just ended a debate "we aren't complicated people, you and I, everything about us has been written, all our pain, our fears, our truths, we've read all the cracks in the life of the other" he lifts my chin, his green eyes glowing in the soft light of bathroom "that's why you weren't afraid of me at the warehouse, even after what you saw, deep down you know we are two parts of the same broken vase".

My words stick in my throat, for all the ways he may be wrong, for all the reasons I should jump up out of this tub and run, there is the very strong fact that he is correct. I was never afraid of him, digging into his past I saw the same scared child that resides within me, the same journey, and the same outcome. The only difference between us is the reason for which we kill, I kill from anger, Areus kills for protection, if we really think about it his moral compass may be brighter than mine. That's not a thought I'm stable enough to have in the midst's of this Stockholm moment. I place my face into the woody nook of his neck, letting his sincerity envelop us in silence, my tired body enjoying the stillness.

The shift of his legs brings my mind from its quiet corner. "Wait here" his voice moves as he rises, stepping from the tub toward the bedroom. I watch the doorway with a noticeable curiosity narrating my face. I don't realize my eyes are closed until they are requested to open by his invitation to join him next to the tub. He uses his body as leverage for my balance as he aides me from the tub. He moves a towel around my body until I'm dry, sliding my arms into a thick robe, wrapping it tightly to keep the chilled air off my skin, he takes my hand, guiding me behind him. The kitchen is twice as big as it could possibly need to be, hunter green cabinets and gold accents, a large island in the middle, marble countertop cascading to the floor. He pulls a bar stool from the counter for me to sit, "what would you like" he makes his way the refrigerator, standing in the open door, moving food around the shelves. "I'm fine" the lie failing me. "What dish is that, Italian" he laughs and I can't help but laugh with him, not at the joke itself but at the adorable pride he felt in making such a stupid joke. He fills his arms with bowls from the fridge, placing them on the island. Strawberries, cantaloupe, grapes, and a fourth bowl hiding its contents beneath a paper towel. He slides the bowls in front of me, pulling something from the drawer into his hand, coming round the island to stool next to mine. He pulls the bowl of strawberries between us, "do you ha" he cuts my words, lifting a clear plastic fork near the smug grin taking over his face, tipping the solid handle toward me for my hand to take. He really has been watching me, the taste of metal hurts my spine, but I only use solid plastic utensils as the ones with the holes in the handles have a weird feel to them that cringes my skin. I take the fork from him, his nose tipping toward the bowl, an obvious instruction for me to eat, pulling the other bowls closer as I take a strawberry slice into my mouth. He watches me closely, stabbing a piece of fruit for me any time I release the fork from my grip "What about you" I whisper, my throat still sore. A small smile lines his lips, his fingers dropping fruit into his mouth, I shift my eyes to his fork, my brow raised at his need for it. "I know it hurts you when people use metal, and that's the only plastic I have" my lips part at the surprise to his attention, his care, "thank you" I coo shyly at him "but after all that I think we can use the same fork". He laughs through a nod, gently taking the fork from my hand, humming at the sweetness of the fruit. "I have something else for you" he pulls the fourth bowl between us, lifting the paper towel, "Honeysuckles" I almost squeak in excitement "when I was in third grade they grew at the fence of the school, I would sneak over at recess and pick some" I lift my eyes to him, his teeth biting his bottom lip through a wide smile "You know this already" I shake my head lightly, removing the voice of that silly little girl from my mind. His hand pulls a honeysuckle from the bowl, "just because I know your stories does not mean I don't want to hear you tell them" he pulls at the stem, bringing it to my lips, I swipe my tongue at the blossom caressing the nectar to my tastebuds. He places the bowls in the sink, turning to lean his hip against the counter, "Come little fox, let's get you to bed" he tips his head to the side toward the bedroom, offering me a set of his pajamas, I decline in favor of the robes softness. He lays on his back, one arm behind his head, one arm out to the side as I mold into him with my head on his bicep in the nook of armpit, my arm wrapping his waist, resting my leg over his thigh. His lips come to rest on my forehead, my eyes closing out the world, nothing to infringe upon my mind except the memory of the night. *Sleep.*

The echo of the gun jerks me awake, the event playing back in my mind, tears gathering in my eyes. I bring my legs over the edge of the bed, gently pulling myself up from his arm, peaking at him over my shoulder. I can't let him see me like this, having my weakness exposed to him is not something I can handle right now. I don't switch on the light, letting my eyes gloss over the dark bathroom, as I walk to the large shower taking up a third of the room, and turn on the water, to warm while I pee. Dropping my robe to the floor I step into the water, humming at the heat as I turn my body under the rain. There's grip of sadness tight in my stomach as my shoulder falls against the wall of the shower, my body sliding to the floor. I wrap my arms around my legs, my forehead hitting my knees, unable to hold back the dam any longer my tears flow freely in the waterfall streaming down on me. My lungs stagger air in through my nose as I pin my bottom lip between my teeth, trying to keep the sound of my whimpers from echoing through the room to Areus. "it's my fault" I whisper to myself as my body rocks back and forth "what have I done, it's my fault".

"Stop it, you didn't do this" his voice suddenly exclaims as he wraps his arms around me, pulling my head to his chest, comforting the willowing weeps falling from my lips. "Cry, little fox, be sad, but don't let Ian weaken you" he consoles me with a brush of my hair from my face. "Don't burry it, use it" his voice shifts, becoming strong and defensive "use it all, every bruise, every break, all the pain. Live in it and let it be your strength" I can hear the devil riding his tongue, his inner child as equally unhealed as mine. *Use it.* My body perks up with a new hope flaming in my mind, I stand so quickly he insists caution, my feet slipping over the tile as I briskly exit the bathroom. I search the room, goosebumps crawling across my wet skin from the cool air, a demand for my attention volumizes his voice as he calls out my name. "Where's my phone" his brows lower with confusion as excitement courses through my smile "I need my phone". "You dropped it when I grabbed you" his shoulders stiffen toward the blades, the fact of the previous day stinging his tongue. "Right" I can't stop the mourning from weighing down on my promise of revenge, *Snap out of it Alex*, I shake the sorrow from my mind. "Okay, well where's your phone?". Annoyance rolls over his face at my question as he raises his hand to his face, pinching the bridge of his nose in a small huff as if he's trying to calm a surfacing shout, "I tossed it on the way here". My hands swing around the room mocking his parental like attitude toward my frustration with a small temper tantrum, "are you kidding me? Damn it Areus, how are" my words are cut by his quiet laugh. He's such an asshole. The urge to punch him clenches my hands to fists as my eyes throw daggers to his chest.

His hand lifts his palm toward me in a sarcastic surrender, his other hand grabbing the blanket from the foot of the bed, "I'm sorry Darlin', you're cute when you fuss". His teeth take in his bottom lip, failing to stifle his continuing laughter as he steps to me wrapping the blanket around my body. Looking down at the covering I'm confronted with the realization of how truly bared I was before him. "Areus" I huff at him, stubbornly holding onto my ire as I grab the blanket from his hands, forcing myself not to enjoy its protection from the cold bite of the room. His hand grabs the side of my neck, the tip of his thumb lifting my chin, meeting my eyes to his as his neck lowers his clenched jaw. "Say it again" his command is rough but soft, the whisper brushing his lips against mine. The urge to feel his tongue in my mouth shivers over my skin as if I was bare to the air again, heat fluttering at my center as confusion shifts my gaze between his eyes, his free hand pressing gently on my lower back, pulling my body into his. "My name was meant for your tongue" his hand grips at my covering tightly as the groan within his whisper tingles moisture between my legs, my walls subconsciously clenching at the thought of him inside me. *Wait.* The possibility that he is making fun of me flushes me with immaturity, a playful satisfaction raising my brow at the idea of denying him of my immediate surrender to his cocky confidence, my tongue pulling my bottom lip between my teeth, crooking a silent *No* at the corner of my mouth. The shape of his eyes become threatening, pupils dilated, as his hand snaps to the back of my head. Tangling my hair in his grip he turns my head to his cheek, his lips to my ear, and mine to his. "Say. It" the strength in his forceful tone send a shock rolling down my spine. My lungs sharply pull in an uncontrolled gasp between the tight teeth of my clenched jaw, my neck fails to pull from his control, though the attempt is weak with false intention. "Areus" I submit softly, the rustic hum of his throat wetting a throb at my core. I part my lips, the tip of my tongue gliding up the edge of his earlobe, his low hum rumbling to a growl as he presses his forehead against mine, his breath filling my mouth through his hovering lips. "I really need a phone" my lids flutter a blink at him. His forehead drops on mine as light laughter stumbles through his nose. His brings his hands to my shoulders, forcing space between us, "kitchen Darlin'". He's doing it again, he's controlling something within himself that wants to break out, like I'm a child he needs to protect from his harshness. He makes me feel small and soft like a baby animal under the large, leafed branches of a tall tree, hiding from the rain. I smile at the gruff sweetness of his gaze as I sweep up the bottom of the blanket, and rush to the kitchen.

"I mean really" I wave the phone at him, disbelief rolling my eyes as I turn the dial of the rotary phone. "Who are you" I raise my palm to stop him, my eyes thinning at him. "Timmy. Yea, its Alex" his brow raises at me as he crosses his arms over his chest impatiently, "shut up Timmy and listen to me. I need a drop for two" I huff my distaste of him and ignore the stress rolling off his words. "Where are we" I whisper to Areus. He shakes his head at me with a long blink, I shake my head back at him with insistence. "Timmy shut up" I shout, tired of his opinions echoing in my ear "just tell management it's Ian Hayes and send the fucking drop". There's a quick shift in Areus' lips, the slight semblance of a smile, apparently he likes when I'm firm, just not with him. "Address" I demand from him through tight teeth, pointing to the phone in my hand. His eyes roll in a blink, a deep inhale puffing his chest as he steps towards me, his clothes still wet from the shower, hugging every muscle, clinging to his half-raised stiffness. My eyes roam his body, a thirst for him biting my bottom lip. He looms over me releasing a sigh from his nose, his tongue pulling his bottom lip between his teeth, watching my eyes devour his silhouette. He clears his throat in demand of my attention. My eyes fly to his, heat flushing my cheeks from the anger in his eyes, "1687 Night Court Rd Carrsville" his voice raised to carry into the phone, his unwavering eye contact quivering my nerves as I confirm Timmy understand the objective, to which he confirms with annoyance "an air drop for two within the hour". I give him a sarcastic "thank you" back as I put the phone down. "The drop will be here in an hour" I shift to move past his intimidation, my step blocked by his arm. "What drop, what are you doing exactly?" his question carries worry, does he think I'm new to this. "We need guns. Ammo. Timmy's an over thinker so there'll probably be a smoke grenade and knives too" I keep my tone flat and definitive as I lower his hand from my stomach, and walk to the bedroom, as a pitched "What" resounds from him. "When it gets here I'll call Ian and". "NO" his voice is strong, demanding, his feet are heavy as he follows me into the room. "By the time he gets here we'll be ready to". "I said NO" the power of his voice flinches my skin, the shock booth alerting and lascivious. My thoughts are rushed with all the ways he could ruin me if I pushed past the self-control he has been granting me. "You don't listen" the deep anger he is echoing through the room pulls me from my daydream, his frustrated hands run through his hair brushing back the loose pieces in his face. "Someone who *knows me so well* should know better than to think I would" I mock his knowledge of me. The smile creeping across my lips is grabbed away by his hand gripping my neck, pulling me into him "This isn't a game Alexandra, I can't put out a fire if you keep sparking it". I grip his wrist, the blanket wrapping me dropping to the floor as I meet my eyes to his. I know I shouldn't push him, shouldn't tempt the devil that lingers in his mind. Drowning any notion of good sense I steady my resolve, "I guess I should find a stronger protector then" my throat strains the words against his grip. His hand pushes harder against my throat, my steps stumbling backwards, slamming my back into the wall beside the bed, "Don't push me Little Fox" his words growl from deep in his throat, my grip tightening around his wrist, his free hand lowering the clingy cloth from his waist. He lifts my thigh, resting my foot on the nightstand "If its attention you're looking for..." he taps his hard tip to my slit, wet with ache "I can deliver that". The rush of his length into my opening draws a heavy gasp into my lungs, my eyes pinching shut at the sudden pain stretching my walls around him. "Fuck" he groans, sliding himself from me, his tip rubbing my slickness over my swelling nub. "MMM. You can get wetter than that Little Fox" the challenge vibrating my core as he leverages a lean against my throat, angling his cock to my crease, driving his full length into me. His hand comes to my thigh, pressing it to the wall, his eyes watching his girth thrust against the pressure of my tight walls, my mouth wide as my lungs fight to pull in air against the grasp of his hand around my neck. My body screams silently within the choke, my pussy weeping from his depth, his force, with the painful pleasure running down my leg. My chest is tight, filled with moans fighting for freedom. "There you go baby" he hums against the dig of my nails into his wrist, my thigh trembling under his hand, my standing leg weakening beneath me "let it go, that's it, I've got you". Tension stiffens my body, my walls throbbing around his relentless depth. "Fuck" he grunts to the ceiling as his thrusts power through the pressure of my orgasm trying to push him from me, "that's it, just like that baby". My core erupts from the graveled tone of his praise, his arms stiffen to increase the hold of his grip as my body gives out beneath me. He pulls his length from, the build gushing onto his tip, "fucking beautiful" his eyes lingering on the flow dripping onto him. He wraps my quaking thigh around his waist, his grip on my throat loosens his hand shifts to the back of my neck, lifting my dangling body into his hold. I bring my hand to the side of his face, my fingers caressing the nape of his neck as I my rest my forehead to his chest. "Oh you're not done yet" he threatens as I slip from his arms, my back hitting the bed. His hands instantly grip my thighs, pulling my ass to the edge of the bed. He reaches for my hands, placing my palms on the backs of my thighs as I lift my head to watch his tip playing at my opening, his arms lifting the wet shirt from his trimmed frame. My head is thrown to the bed as he dives into me, my eyes rolling closed, a heavy inhale filling my lungs. He reaches forward, gripping my hair as he lifts my back off the bed "go ahead baby, watch how good you're doing". My eyes open to the sight of his thick length pounding quickly into the fade of my pussy, my breaths hard with the crunched position of my body cutting my lung capacity. My nails dig into the soft flesh of my thighs at the building climax, my eyes shutting out the sweet sight of him stretching me full. My head falls to the bed with a sudden relief of pain, my chest heaving at the rush of air as he slides himself from me, "not yet baby" he claps his shaft on my clit, "fuck" I breathe into a hum. He gently slides his hands under mine, releasing my nails from the burrows they dug, pressing my thighs down wide, gliding his glistening cock over my sensitive jewel. My teeth pinch down on my bottom lip, his moan drenching my senses. He leans forward, baring his weight down on my thighs, sliding his shaft inside me, reaching his limit with the pumped thrust of his base. He withdraws from me slowly, driving his tip into me again, popping another thrust at his base. It's a pleasure I've never felt before, slow but powerful, the repetition rushing my arms above my head, hands gripping the sheet, my elbows together hiding my face as my teeth clench around my bicep, forcing down the sounds begging to ring out my ecstasy. My body hardens, quaking my thighs forcefully against his palms, "pllleeeaase" I sing softly through my bite. "Speak up baby, I can't hear you" he growls increasing the tempo of his thrusts, my arm falling from my gapping mouth. "Look at me" his command pinch my eyes shut, embarrassed to be so exposed to him "look at me Darlin'" he whispers softly, but commanding. I let my eyes open to meet his, "tell what you need" I whimper at the rough desperation drawn on his face as he increases the power behind his thrusts, *FUCK I didn't know pain could be so pleasurable*, my brows raise to a furrow, begging him silently to finish me. "I need your voice Alexandra" his rustic whimper breaks my resolve, my screaming moans powering him into me. His grip bruising my thighs as my walls clench and throb around his girth, the build of my climax seeping from my stretched opening. "Oh fuck," he groans slamming into me faster than I can pull air into fill my lungs, "there's my good girl" his feral whimpers wrap my gasping yelps like candied syrup. I grip the sheet tightly, my nails digging into my palm through the fabric, my other hand wrapping around my throat, my orgasm flowing over his veined shaft as he thrusts his sweet emission into my thirsty depths, the warmth pushing me past my climax, my body quivering beneath him, my breath caught in my throat. He rests a final thrust in me at depth, a hum rumbling his throat as I pulsate around him, my hands relaxing as my chest heaves with brisk breaths, a numbness settling in my legs. He slides his length from my gripping slit, our nectar trailing my ass, drenching the sheet beneath me. I sit up slowly, my body aching, my printed thighs jellied, as he kneels between my legs, hands brushing my hair to the back, gripping the sides of my neck. "I know you can take care of yourself, but I'd never recover if you get hurt going after Ian before you're not ready" his eyes look into mine with severity. "You speak as if you couldn't live without me" I chuckle dismissively. "I would survive without you, yes, but it would not be a life" the power is gone from his voice as his thumb caresses my cheek, drowning me with a realization that I want to feel like this forever, cared for, needed, and safe. I want to be his forever. He kisses my forehead as he stands and fades into the bathroom, the rush of water splashing into the tub luring my mind back to reality. I stumble to my feet, my staggered steps carrying my tired body to the bathroom, concern fills his eyes at the sight of me. He takes my hands, leading me to the tub, "I would have carried you" he says helping me balance on his strength as I lift my legs into the tub, lowering myself into the hot water. Resting my head back as the steam swirling around me fills my nose with rose and vanilla. I'm still surprised at the amount of attention he gave to the details as he watched me, it's no wonder I'm so enthralled with him, he's got the main source codes to my fundamental make up. "Close your eyes" an instruction I'm all too pleased to follow, allowing him a moment to shower. The water from the shower stops, and I can hear the clap of his wet feet on the tile coming towards me. His hand enters the water, the soft sponge caressing my skin as the sincerity of his care washes away my embarrassment of the raw carnal pleasure he just took from me. "Come" his tone wraps the command in silk as he offers his hand, supporting me from the tub. He softly wipes the dampness from my skin and leads me to the bed, I flinch at the soreness of my tender opening meeting the mattress, "I'm fine" I offer in response to the uncontrolled sound of discomfort that pulled his gaze to me over his shoulder. He continues to the chair by the window, where he's gathered my clothes. He brings the pile to the bed and gently dresses me, before stepping back to the chair to dress himself as my eyes watch the clock on the bedside table, *three am. Damn, what time did I call Timmy.* "You should sleep" his sensitivity envelops me as he comes to the bed beside me. "Do you remember", the ring of the phone from the kitchen halts my question, "It's here" I rise to my feet, hauling my soft legs toward the front door. Opening the door, I step on to the porch, my eyes searching the sky for the drop. "Evening" the familiar voice wafting on the breeze turns my gaze to his barrel.

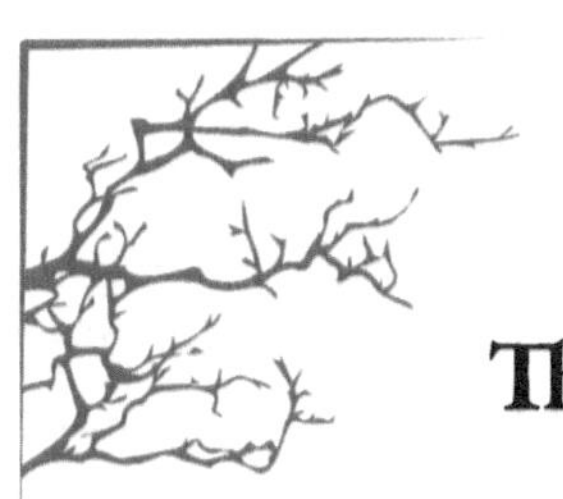

The Bodyguard

"That was quick" I tease, the close of the door rising me from the bed. Coming around the corner from the hallway to the foyer I'm affronted with the heart stopping vision of Ian holding Alexandra's arm firmly, Connelly pointing a gun at her back. I'm sure Scarlett and Silver are circling the cabin in search of setups. "You two should really pick better friends" he scoffs smugly as he points between Alexandra and I, "*Tim* was far too easy to buy". I knew it was a mistake to let her make that call. I bite back the urge to demand he release her, there's no reasoning with Ian once he's made up his mind. My hands clench into fists begging to be swung through his chest. "Careful brother" he threatens, his hand pulling a knife from his back, resting the tip of the blade under her chin. Suddenly I'm weak, all my skill, all my power rendered useless, Connelly will shoot her without hesitation if I so much as move too quickly. "We don't have to do this" my warning is calm only for the sake of keeping myself from acting too hastily, my eyes fixed on my little fox. "No we didn't have to do this, but you let this bitch get in your head" he taps the point of the blade to his temple "for what? Pussy?" he laughs out, "two weeks, you could have taken her at any time" he shifts the knife running the sharp metal over her lips. "Don't" I shift forward with demand. His arm is swift, drawing a gasp from her as the knife digs into the floor before my feet. "Oh, shit, I get it, you did take her" his laughter barks out as he pulls her in front of him, "I knew she liked it rough" he mocks, his arms wrapping her waist, her neck, pulling her back against his body. She stiffens under his grip attempting to keep distance between them "Get the fuck off me" she protests through clenched teeth, her voice strained under his ill pressured grip on her neck. Ian's hand drops from her waist, cupping between her legs, his lips to her ear "I like a fighter". She juts her head from his whisper, her eyes pinching out the pain of her neck twisting against his ungiving grip. Her eyes meet mine, ignited and reckless, *Don't do it,* I shake my head at her softly, she has to know I would die before I let him hurt her. "How sweet" my eyes roll from hers to his through the sarcasm leeching from his mouth, "I *was* gonna just put you both down clean and quick" he reaches around his back, bringing a gun forward "but I think I'd rather have a little fun first" he aims the gun at my chest. He must be kidding, his audacity is high right now, did he suddenly forget who I am, what I've done for less. He will die tonight, even if the last thing I do. She pulls against his hold, trying to free herself from his clutch, "How long do you think she'll last" his evil intent rides a smile across his lips. I look to Connelly, his arms stiffening his aim to her against the anger in my eyes. "Ian" I lift my arms, offering my palms in placating surrender as I step forward. My steps quickly ceased by the sound of the gun, the burn above my heart pulling my eyes to the red waterfall staining my shirt. Droplets splash my face as a second shot tunnels through my shoulder dropping me to a knee. Alexandra screams an objection, the fear in her voice refocusing my blurred attention to her. She has one hand pulling at his arm for release the other reaching out to me, "Areus" her voice echoes through the ringing in my ears. My eyes blink tightly. "Areus, look at me" her smile is tense as my eyes meet hers. "I am safe with you, yes or no?" her is voice begging me to find my strength. I strengthen my resolve and rise to my feet, "Yes" her smile brightening at my stance and affirmation. "I am yours, yes or no?" she is trying to power me through the short heaving breaths in my chest at the pain of the blood leaking from my body. "Yes" I stand strong, posturing confidence at Ian. "And you are mine, yes or no?" the softness of her voice rushes my eyes over face, a part of her questioning my answer. I swallow down the blood in my throat, firming my voice, I need to be sure her faith will never waiver from the truth, "Always". Her face brightens, crooking a smile from the corner of my mouth. Ian's face curls with distain, his arm hardening for the next shot. Her head snaps back a hard connection to Ian's face, her elbow coming to his nose without hesitation, the gun falling from his hand as he stumbles back from his lost grip over her. She spins a quick turn, grabbing the barrel in Connelly's hand, throwing two jabs to the center of his face, as his hand falls from the trigger. She steps back, using her body as a barricade between them and me, her arms extending the guns aim at Ian. She's faster than I gave her credit for. Ian wipes at the blood flowing from his nose, his tongue cleaning it from his lips, as Connelly steadies his stance beside him. "Your father was a piece of shit child rapist. Your mother did the world a favor" her fearless boast rolls a stiffening pride over my length, my body ready to appreciate her through any pain. Scarlett and Silver step in from the sitting room beside Ian, circling behind me like hyena.

She peeks over her shoulder at their position, letting her gaze rest on Scarlett for a moment, "but you knew about your fathers acquired tastes though, right Ian?". Her voice stiffens under the reveal as her eyes shift back to him "it's a taste you've recently shared together". *What, no, he wouldn't.* My eyes search his face hoping that for all his sins raping a child would not be one of them. Ian's stare on her is cold, his smile rough through a rage clenched jaw, "What can I say" his brown raises tauntingly "it's a delicacy". My stomach knots as Connelly shifts beside Ian protectively. How could I have been so blind to what was happening. "Don't" the sharpness of her tone locks onto Connelly like a sniper, watching him intently as he looks to Ian for instruction. Ian has his eyes pinned on her, an evil smiling drawing across his face, taunting her peripheral, as he ticks his head up. The sound of the gun instantly follows his invisible order, a clean shot to the center of Connelly's forehead, her aim steadfast to Ian, watching the smile fall from his face at the thud of Connelly's body hitting the floor as a devilish pride pulls the corners of my mouth into a smile. Scarlett and Silver rustle behind me, I look back at each of them, guns pointed, "Alexandra" I call out weakly, "Its okay" her assurance is calm and strong. Ian laughs "You're out numbered baby". He's arrogant but he's right, and I'm not sure how I'm going to get her out of this. "But I know something you don't" I can hear a smile pulling her lips as she whispers the strong conviction at him. "What's that" Ian softly mocks an underestimating challenge at her. "Your father made the mistake of promising he would stop". "Promised who" he chuckles out with disbelief. Tension grabs my nerves, blood loss slowing the world as she lowers her arms relaxingly to her side. "Scarlett". The revelation hits my chest like an arrow. My widened eyes throw shock toward Scarlett, their face calmly holding a demon's smile. The echo of the gun stings my ear, as the surprise of the moment levels me to my knees. Alexandra's stance remains firm as a second bullet brushes past her hair, the two shots mining through Ian's chest and head in tandem, his buckling body stumbles back, falling smoothly to the floor as my weakened mind fails to pull understanding from my memory. Alexandra kneels before me, her hand softly on my face. The questions rushing through my mind are halted by her lips caressing mine, our tongues swirling gently together. "I like her boss" Silver cuts in unphased by the events of the night, his unexpected words pull my lips from Alexandra's kiss. I'd laugh if I hadn't just been affronted with such ruinous knowledge. "What?" he steps toward my question to my side, his eyes smile at Alexandra as he sweeps his hand under my arm, assisting me to my feet. "Strong", once again I am met with pride as Silver offers approval of her through his brisk word. He moves around Alexandra, stepping to Ian's body and swiftly jerks the chain from around his neck. I watch the steadiness of Silver's face as he wraps the chain around my wrist, the key to the safe on the boat dangling at my pinky. "Slainte" he endears as he releases my hand, a nod exchanged between him and Alexandra.

The loss of blood drops my body into Alexandra's hands, in all that's happened I'd almost forgotten I'd been shot. "Kitchen" Scarlett enforces from behind me. The three of them aide me to the large island, their hands scurrying over me, pulling the drenched shirt from my body. There's no hesitation between my back meeting the cold island top and the burning pour of alcohol over the holes in my skin, Silver's elevated voice instructs Alexandra to control my shoulders. Her hands press me into the marble surface as Silver's fingers dive into my torn flesh, fishing for the bullet planted beneath the surface, my jaw clenching tightly, stifling my pained growl. I am offered no ease form the clink of the metal against the floor as my agitated wounds are met with the familiar sting of the cruel liquid again. He slides a hand beneath me, lifting my back from the slab, hitting a towel to my shoulder with a terse instruction to press it to my wound. His lack of delicacy makes me want to punch him in the face. I swing my legs over the edge of the island finding myself in need of air as a wooziness leans my body against the bloody counter. I pull a deep breath and steady myself against my mind. "Anyone care to explain".

Scarlett and Silver look over my shoulder to Alexandra, their eyes following her as she walks around the island to complete our circle. "My deep dive into all of you led me to Scarlett's hospital reports, it was so close to Tristan taking them in that all the reports listed self-infliction, a symptom of trauma, ptsd, but I knew better, I knew what left all those burns, bruises, and bleeding" her lowered brows offer sympathy to Scarlett through the similarities of her own trauma, "And if you knew why Riosin hired me then so did Scarlett. When I had aim on Ian I saw them outside the window, it would have been a clean shot to take me out but they didn't even drawn their gun, that's when I knew they understood. Scarlett earned that shot, and I knew if I had the chance to reveal Ian's hand in his father's actions, it was a shot they would take." "Sly little fox" I chuckle through a proud smile, the endearment flushing her cheeks. I look down at myself, marred and bloody, my eyes drawing once again to the key, the symbolism of Silver's allegiance passing to me "you don't have to stay, take it, take it all and go". Silver and Scarlett both sharpen their posture, "Ireland is nice this time year" Scarlett speaks to the ground. I twist the chain from my wrist, steadying my stance from the island, offering the key to them with full acceptance. Alexandra comes to my side, smiles of understanding between her and Scarlett, *I'm missing something again.* "Perfect for a family vacation" Scarlett invites, closing my hand around the key. I sigh a laugh from my nose not wanting to overly tenderize the moment.

"Fuck" I shift the subject as I take in the state of the cabin, grabbing up the vodka bottle "I actually liked this place" I take down a gulp, the burn in my throat easy to manage in comparison to the events of this night. I throw the bottle into the foyer, the flammable liquid splashing their bodies as the glass shatters between Ian and Connelly. Alexandra steps to the stove, releasing a hiss as she twists the knobs. "We have a plane to catch" she boasts grabbing a bottle of whiskey from the counter and twisting off the cap. Holding the tipped bottle lazily in her hand, the liquid trails behind her as she walks to the door carelessly stepping over Ian. She throws the bottle down the hall by the bedroom door, licking the remanence of the liquor from her finger, something devilish is lurking in her smile, and I love her for it. She turns her gaze to us, sweet, and soft, "We take care of each other, yes or no?". She looks to Silver first as he sharpens his stance against the phrase of the question she previously endeared me with, the invitation into her heart not lost on him, "Yes" his response is strong with promise. Scarlett steps forward attracting her attention "Yes" they offer without doubt or hesitation. She shifts her eyes to mine, she already knows, of course, but she needs to hear it, "Always, little fox". Her lips pull into an accomplished smile, the duality of her soul embodying the power of Athena. Quite the family she has created here, broken, and damaged, but strong. "Always" she copies back to me. I look to Silver and Scarlett, tipping my head toward the door, following behind them out the room. They continue out of the cabin to their car, resting against the hood, Alexandra steps out to porch, while I riffle through Connelly's pocket for his keys and the lighter I know he has. Pulling my hand from his wet clothes I step back to meet Alexandra's side, the flick of my wrist flinging back the lighter's lid as my thumb strikes the metal, igniting the spark. I toss the small flare into the flammable puddle between Ian and Connelly. The fire rolls over their bodies as Alexandra takes my hand, leading us down the porch stairs to meet Silver and Scarlett by their car. We calmly watch the flames make their way to the kitchen, "So Ireland huh" I joke at Scarlett, the four of us unphased by the combustion of the gas as it knocks glass from the windows. "It's where we are from" Scarlett's steady words swing my eyes from the burning cabin. Neither Scarlett, nor Silver, have ever spoken of where they came from, and the immense trust they just laid over us is not lost on me, a trust I will protect even in death. "Looks like we're gonna need passports" Alexandra chimes at Scarlett happily, she slaps her palms to the hood of the car pushing herself off in excitement, a dancing a spin to face us, "just one stop first" the corner of her mouth crooking into a devil ridden smile.

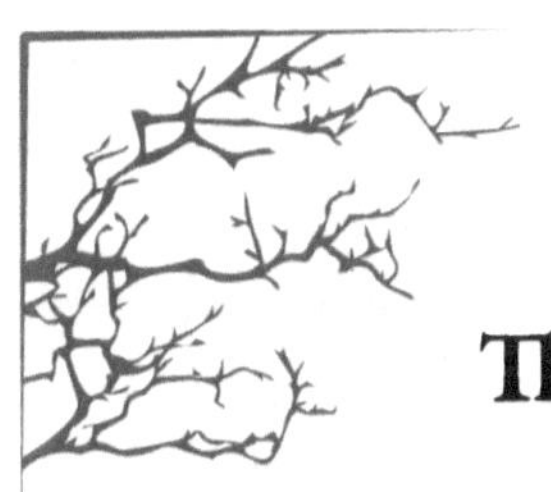

The Accountant

"Room service for Smith" my voice feigns pleasantry as I stand before the door, Areus behind me, Scarlett and Silver to either side of the door. A stifled rustling echoes into the hallway, "Coming" he sings. The door opens to a tall well framed man in a black suit, at least Timmy put all that worry to good use and hired bodyguards. His mouth is too busy asking me who I am that he is not paying attention to the gun in my hand as a silent shot to his knee pulls him to the ground. "two" a second shot to his head from Areus cuts off his uneducated warning to the others. Stepping over him I turn the corner to see Timmy poorly attempting to conceal himself from me, sitting on the sofa behind two more bodyguards whose guns are aimed loosely toward me. I raise my hands pretending surrender, "put it down" the taller one demands. "Come on boys, I'm just here to see a friend" I mock, their aim stiffening at the obvious bullshit falling from my lips, the barrels following the shift of my body as I lower my gun to the floor and kick it to him with my foot. "I know you're here, join us" Timmy's voice omits a newfound sense of self as he speaks his command to the space behind me. Areus steps in the room, to my side, raised arms offering empty palms to the aim of the shorter guard who's requesting a gun from him. Areus moves his arm behind him slowly, pulling the gun from his back to the ground and kicks it over to the short guard. "Got em'?" he questions, shifting to retrieve the gun at his feet, passing it behind him to Timmy as he stands. "Get it" he cues to the taller guard, stiffening his aim back on Areus as the taller guard bend for retrieval of my gun and passes it back to Timmy as well. "Seems we've both made some changes" Timmy sits forward resting his elbows on his knees, his wrists dangling the guns between his legs "you look *good*" his inflection carries a poor attempt to taunt me. I look down at my well fitted black suit, suede accents on the lapels and pocket slits, donned over a low-cut black waistcoat, and suede black loafers. Like Jidenna said *I don't want my best dressed day in casket,* "What can I say, it's my villain arc" my lack of concern for his intimidation evident in my playful tone. Timmy steps forward between the men, his arms at his side, a gun resting halfheartedly in each hand "I'm really sorry about Jessyca, you have to understand" his brows are furrowed and his mouth is frowned but his eyes hold no sense of care, he doesn't actually feel any sense of remorse. "Nothing" I cut in, the audacity of this so-called man to even think he can pull sympathy from me "I have to understand nothing". "I've spent years at that company enduring the aftermath of careless bullshit from the two of you" he raises his arm, aiming my gun at me "I was given an opportunity and I took it, just like this" he pulls the trigger twice, winching at the click. Scarlett steps into the room beside me, Silver beside Areus, guns aimed with intent at the bodyguards. I suck my teeth at his misfortune "empty" I sigh out "you think I'd give you a loaded gun" soft laughter angering his gaze. "But the" the burning numbness in his hand halts his words as the gun falls to the floor. "Your mistake was having only three guards, one bullet in each of our guns is more than enough against that" I can't help but smile at the shock freezing on his face, his stiff steps stumbling backward "but what you really should have focused on" I wiggle my fingers to shift his attention to my hand "is why I'm wearing gloves", his eyes grow wide as his body falls back to the couch. Scarlett and Silver each deliver a shot to the brain of a guard as I step between them to Timmy, shifting his flopped body on the sofa, positioning his back straight up and his face forward. Sitting across from him on the coffee table I pull the gloves from my hands, placing them beside me with a sigh "you never did give any credit to poison control" I lean over the side of the table picking up my gun by the silencer, "poneratoxin" I turn the handle to his eyes, revealing my ring cut and soldered to it. "Non-lethal, unfortunately" Areus chuckles out, mocking the statement I once used on him, and I can feel the brightness he brings to my eyes as I take in his smile. "True" I emphasize with a playful point to Areus as I look back to the immobilized man before me, placing the gun on the table "That won't kill you". I reach into the inner pocket of my jacket, pulling a syringe into his view "but this will". I lean forward, my free hand pulling his wrist, lengthening his arm to me "you know what happens when you inject even the smallest air bubble into the bloodstream" I rest the covered point on the skin of his inner elbow, "nothing" I laugh relief toward him as I drop his rubbery arm to the sofa. "The truth is in most cases an air bubble in the bloodstream will generally be filtered out in the lungs causing no actual harm", I pull the plastic from the needle and draw air into the length of the cylinder, looming the threat in the air between us, watching his eyes take in the instrument of his impending demise. "But" I swiftly drive the metal tip into his chest "when you inject it into the heart" I lean forward positioning myself in the center of his sights "it can't pump through" my thumb presses the air into his heart. The world slows as water builds across his lower lids, I know he can feel it, his heart trying to pump the empty ventricle.

I release the syringe, placing my hand on his cheek I wipe a single tear from under his left eye. I begin the download of this moment into my core memory, fixed closely on the teared eye as his pupil widens over the light brown iris. I pull my hand to my stomach in relief, a smile forming as my eyes close, imagining Jessyca playfully complaining about the cleanup and the paperwork.

The warmth of a hand under my chin, lifting my face, draws my eyes open "we've got you little fox" Areus coos tapping my chin with instruction to stand. I rise quickly to the tips of my toes, my hand at the nape of his neck, roughly meeting our lips together, my parted mouth hungry for his tongue. He grips my hair, pulling my lips from his, I sense a sweetness coming to his mind, something telling him I need softness, like after Jessyca died. My mind shadows lasciviously, I don't want his tender falter, I want him feral. "You don't have to say anything" I lick at his lip, his eyes watching my mouth "some men just can't function around death". He tilts his head, "I wouldn't taunt, little fox" his jaw clenching around the words as his eyes roam within mine in search of a submission he won't find. "We all have our limits" I test, his eyes narrow at the bratty smile pulling my lip into my teeth. His grip in my hair tightens, tugging my neck, trapping a chuckle in my throat. I can feel his hand between us, undoing the confines of his pants, "Boys, would you be so kind as to wait for us in the hall" a threatening tone drips from the polite words, I pushed him too far, I may regret it, but it'll be the most pleasurable of regrets. "Of course" Silver responds, amusement wavering the tone of his words. Areus maneuvers at my pants, his unwavering eyes contact building anticipation within me as the fabric falls to my ankles. With the click of the door closing Scarlett and Silver on the other side his grip in my hair twists my neck, my feet tangled in my pants and stumbling as he half drags me around the couch, forcing my chest down on ledging of the back of the sofa, his grip in my hair turning my eyes to Timmy's frozen face, his other hand shifting his pants, his cock thumping my clit as his hand grabs my waist, while the kick of his foot separates my legs, "Is this what you wanted" he dives into me at full speed, I cry out at the lack of moisture burning against the stretch of his girth. He retreats to his tip, my lungs too tight to breath as he pushes his length inside me again, his depth rumbling a grunt in both our throats. "Does it hurt" he pulls back, "mmhhmm" I muffle, my lips pressed between my teeth, forcing my lungs to try to take in air through my nose. "Louder" he commands, smashing into me again, my eyes pinching shut, "Does. It. Hurt, little fox" his voice is soft though the question is firmed with dominion. I force my lips from my teeth, "yes" wavers from me in a whimper. "Good" his voice is hard, powering his quickened pace, relentlessly thrusting into my core, moans falling from my wide mouth as his painful length pulls me inside out. "Open your eyes baby" he loosens his grip in my hair bringing his palm to the nape of my neck, wrapping his grip "I said open your eyes, look at him" he pulls in his digits, the pressure stopping the air in my lungs, breaking my resolve as my submission slicks his staff, "watching you end him was beautiful" his affirmation drips my climax from his swollen spheres. "Fuck, that's it baby, mmhhmm, let it go" his whimpering moans pushing me past my rise "don't push me out, keep going baby" my center throbs against his continued gruff whimpers as he thrusts into my clenching orgasm. The increased power of his drive shifts the sofa beneath me, dropping Timmy's bouncing head to my shoulder. "Pl...please" I stammer. His grip pulls my neck, bringing my ear up to his lips, dropping the face of the corpse to the seat of the couch, his free hand pressing an arch into my back "please what" his moan whispers in my ear, "fuuuuck" I sigh out against his angled thrusts pounding a new build at me core, "use your words baby" his hand shifts forward over my throat, regaining control of my lungs, "pl...c..m for m.." I beg through gasps "good girl" he growls "you want me to cum for you little fox?" his whisper echoes in my ear as his merciless pace catches my screams under his grip around my throat. My quivering legs begin to weaken beneath me, my climax wetting his pelvis "MMM" he hums loudly pulling back on my neck "fuck, that'll make me cum baby" his cheek pressed against mine, his moans flowing into my gapped mouth. My legs fall, his grip around my throat the only thing holding me up, while his hand reaches around to my center, his fingertips caressing my button with each thrust. His grip on my neck silencing my screams, depriving my lungs of air, my muscles tighten with pleasure, convulsing around the speed of his depth, "oh god baby, that's it" his sweet words stammering a gruff whimper, my quivering walls milking his throbbing cock. He pulls my neck down, releasing his grip, as he steps forward, dropping my face to the chest of the body laid on the sofa. One hand gripping my waist steadying my balance above the back of the sofa, my feet pressing into his calves at the lack of security, as he pumps into me like a lifeless doll, his other hand circling my swollen nub with our overflow. My screams are stifled by the force of him burying my face into the demised chest beneath me as I attempt to beg his mercy, the shirt of our conquest tearing at the tightness of my grip. "Give me one more baby" his command ignoring my muffled pleas. My lungs freeze with ecstasy as my fists press against lifeless flesh, my body lifting and bending into itself around the sofa back, "fuuuuuuck" I sing in through a clenched breath, my climax rolling back my eyes, "ooohhh fuck" he coos as the force of my grip slides the dead man's frame off the edge of the sofa, my body falling forward, submitting me to a new angle of his depth. "That's it, let me hear you baby" his whimper grunting a harmony to my screams as his cock pounds his thick nectar into my core. He sucks air through his teeth, slowing his thrusts, chuckling through a moan as he slides his length from my ruin. I can hear the shuffle of his body behind me, tucking himself back into his pants, as I weakly attempt to settle to my feet. "I've got you little fox" the return of his softness shifting me into his body, my bent knees holding my body to him as he carries me to the small kitchen, my entrance dripping into the sink as he rests me on the ledge, starting a flow of water. He cups his hand under the faucet behind me, bringing little handfuls of water between my legs, rinsing his emission from me, his fingertips roaming over my sensitive gem, a hum of pleasure dropping my forehead to his chest. He lifts my chin, caressing a slow kiss upon my lips. Reaching over he lays out a towel, carefully placing me on it he does his best to dry me, it's not perfect but it sweet. He lifts me off the counter to my feet, going down on a knee he repositions my pants, lifting them to my waist and putting me back together. Looking down at him I neatly brush stray hair from his face, and suddenly I'm rushed with the realization that I'm going to fall in love with this man. He stands, his arms pulling me into his chest, my arms wrapping his waist wanting to hold on to the sound of his heart forever. "You're going to marry me one day, yes or no?" his question is simply knowledge he needs reinforced. I look up at him, resting my chin on his chest, his eyes taking in the shape of my fac, "Yes", his appreciation of my softness blushing my cheeks through a lip bitten smile. I walk to the coffee table grabbing up our guns and my gloves, taking one last look at the pathetic corpse on the floor. Areus steps behind me "don't worry darlin' there's so much bad in the world" he rests a kiss on my neck "we will kill them all" his whisper chills the dampness lingering on my skin from his lips as the promise of forever cleansing the world together flushes my senses. "Areus?" I turn to face him. "Darlin?" he playfully mocks back. I slide my hand up his chest to the back of his neck "when we get on the plane". "Mmhhmm". I pull his ear to my lips "I want you to split me apart". He groans lasciviously through his nose as his hand grabs my chin. He brings my mouth to his as his thumb parts my lips, his tongue tangling desire on my taste buds. "Yes ma'am".